JAKE LOGAN

SLOCUM AND THE OUTLAW'S TRAIL

BERKLEY BOOKS, NEW YORK

SLOCUM AND THE OUTLAW'S TRAIL

A Berkley Book/published by arrangement with
the author

PRINTING HISTORY
Berkley edition/June 1989

ISBN: 0-425-11618-2

A BERKLEY BOOK ® TM 757,375
Berkley Books are published by The Berkley Publishing Group,
200 Madison Avenue, New York, N.Y. 10016.
The name "BERKLEY" and the "B" logo
are trademarks belonging to Berkley Publishing Corporation.

PRINTED IN THE UNITED STATES OF AMERICA

10 9 8 7 6 5 4 3 2 1

SLOCUM AND THE
OUTLAW'S TRAIL

1

John Slocum stared out of the bouncing stagecoach at the parched land and the towering cliffs. The sky looked scorched and brassy, and the hot air shimmered. Not as restful to look at as the filly sitting opposite him in the coach, Slocum thought. She was busty and brazen, with flirty dark eyes in a pretty face. Her name was Honey, and Slocum found her rightly named.

But he found another passenger, Jared Cooper, all wrong: a pig-eyed, bulky rancher with a mean, tight mouth who made sour comments to the other passengers, smoked a rotten cigar, and bragged that he owned the biggest longhorns in the territory. He wore a Colt in a well-used holster. When he discovered Slocum was a Georgia man who had fought under General Pickens, he said with his mean grin, "You Rebs never had a chance."

Slocum was on the verge of sternly admonishing him when the stage tilted crazily. The driver yelled, jerking the reins so sharply that Slocum was thrown against Honey. But for Slocum, any sudden stop on a stage called for a fast gun move. He glanced out.

They were in a narrow pass where the stagecoach wheel had hit one of several rocks, apparently loosened from the upper cliff by a recent rain.

The driver, cursing softly, climbed down, stared at the rocks, then started to lug them to the side.

"Reckon we might lend a hand," Slocum said.

There were two men in business suits—Fowler, who was gray-eyed and stout, and Lucas, who was dark-eyed and slender—also traveling in the stage, and all climbed out to look at the rocks and the slightly jarred wheel. The scorching sun beat down hard on the pitted cliff nearby.

Slocum and the businessmen set about carrying the rocks off to the side. Jared Cooper watched with a smile, lazily lighting another cigar. Honey gazed at him with distaste. "Don't exert yourself, Cooper."

His small eyes glinted, and he stretched. "I didn't buy a ticket on this stage to lift any stones."

They had cleared most of the stones when they heard a low penetrating voice. "Don't anyone move."

They turned to look at the slender, sinewy man in a black mask who had slipped from behind a break in the cliff. He held a gun and looked easy as he came forward. "Now, don't anyone try be a hero. Not worth it."

Slocum studied the masked man coming toward them. He looked young and fast. His blue eyes

gleamed through the mask. His voice had a smooth silky tone, not what you'd expect from a desperado.

Cooper looked sullen, despising the fact that such a youngster would try to push a man like him around. "Listen, sonny, you don't know who you're messin' with. How far do you figger to get before we put a posse on you?"

The masked youngster stared at him, saying nothing.

Cooper figured he had nailed the yearling's attention with the right words, and he pushed on. "Who are you, the Masked Kid? I'd hightail outa here, if I was you, while I was still undamaged."

The Kid's mouth, which showed under the mask, twisted in a funny way. He turned to Slocum and the driver, who were wearing Colts. "You two, drop your guns." His voice was harsh.

Slocum felt almost amused at this young desperado. There was something about him—he was almost gentlemanly and didn't sound like a robber. What the hell did he want? Slocum would drop his gun and see what happened. He'd met killers of all kinds, and this one didn't fit the groove. Slocum felt more curiosity than anything else.

The Masked Kid kicked the guns behind him, then walked directly in front of Cooper, who still had his gun in its holster. He stared hard at Cooper but seemed to be thinking of something else. "You're Jared Cooper."

Cooper was surprised. "That's right. Reckon you know me. So I say again, if I were you I'd head for the hills fast."

With a quick move, the Kid hit Cooper's cheek

with his pistol. It wasn't a hard blow, but it sent Cooper back a step and left a red welt on his cheek.

Cooper bit his lip in fury. It seemed crazy, a kid doing this to him. "Mighty brave, little fella. Hiding behind a mask and got a gun on me."

The Masked Kid stared at him, his blue eyes glittering like ice. "Why do you remind me of a rattlesnake? Not even that, because a rattler gives you warning."

The words didn't make much sense to Cooper. What the hell did that mean—warning? But more important, he still had his gun. Did the Kid forget it? If he could only get the right moment to pull it. Maybe he could stall. "What the hell you talkin' about, boy? What warning?"

"You've got a minute to figger it out."

"What d'ya mean—figger what out? Who are you?"

The blue eyes gleamed behind the mask. "Think about it, Cooper. Now, I'm gonna put my gun in my holster. After that you've got thirty seconds to draw."

Jared Cooper scowled, trying to understand what was happening, what the kid was talking about. Something vague went through his mind, but it didn't stick, for he shook his head. The main thing was, this sawed-off runt was giving him a shot, and if he couldn't outdraw him, he'd be a monkey's uncle.

Then a queer streak went through Cooper. To be picked for the draw—why was the Kid doing it? Cooper didn't know him from a mud fence. And

what did he mean about giving warning? His face paled as a thought came to him.

Time was running out. They were watching, the filly and the Reb, to see his guts. Well, he'd show them red-hot action. The seconds were ticking, the Kid was waiting, dreaming, and Cooper, going for the edge, streaked for his Colt. He had it out of the holster and the Kid hadn't even moved. A thrill of power went through Cooper as he started the gun up. Then he saw a blur of movement and a spit of yellow fire from the gun barrel. He felt himself flung back as the bullet pierced his heart. He fell in slow motion, slipping to the ground like an emptying bag of sawdust. He lay there, remembering. Then he died.

Looking down at the dead man, something seemed to have gone out of the Masked Kid. A restless move from Honey brought him out of his trance.

Lucas was pale as a ghost and ready to throw his wallet. Fowler's lips twitched with fear.

The Kid looked at them calmly—at Honey, at Slocum. Then he picked up the guns on the ground, emptied the bullets, and tossed the guns back.

"You can ride now," he said in a muted voice, gun in hand, watching.

Lucas looked startled, feeling suddenly hopeful about his stuffed wallet.

The stage driver, Casey, was astonished, too, but he didn't hesitate. He holstered his gun, climbed to his seat, and waited for his passengers to move into the coach. Slocum looked at the Kid, and the icy blue eyes behind the mask met him straight on.

Casey whacked the whip, the horses strained, and the springs creaked as the stagecoach lurched forward.

Slocum glanced out the window. The Masked Kid was still watching them. Then he looked down at the dead man.

The Cragg City stagecoach bounced along the trail, and for a time, the passengers sat in silence.

Finally, Honey spoke. "Well, what do you make of that?"

Slocum shook his head. "Mighty strange."

Fowler's beefy red face looked disbelieving. "Never thought it would go like that. Surely thought he was after our money. Didn't you, Lucas?"

Lucas wore a derby, a shoelace tie, and a tight striped suit. He shrugged. "Why else would a gunslinger stop a coach?"

Fowler thought about it. "Looked like a youngster. Not a hardened desperado. Not yet."

Honey took a breath. "Well, I didn't think much of Cooper. But it was a miserable way to go. A short and happy life for our friend Cooper. Dad won't like it."

"So your dad won't like it." Lucas was satirical. "If you'll pardon my saying so, miss, Cooper acted mighty dumb. He kept threatening the Kid holding a gun. Don't you think so, Mr. Slocum?"

Slocum rubbed his chin. "Cooper had his gun. He didn't have to eat humble pie."

Honey looked at Slocum. "But weren't you surprised? I mean, he just shot Cooper. He didn't even rob us."

Slocum looked out of the stage at the dusty brush. A buzzard was flying lazily toward the massive canyon in the distance. "The Kid set up the ambush. Those rocks didn't appear by accident. He planted them."

They all stared at him.

Then Honey said, "But he meant to stop us for robbery. And he got sidetracked because Cooper insulted him. Isn't that what happened?"

Slocum smiled. "Reckon you'll have to ask the Kid. I reckon he knew what he was after."

Lucas looked puzzled. "So why didn't he shoot Cooper straight off? Why take the chance of the draw?"

"You'd'a done it like that, hey, Lucas?" Fowler grinned.

"Bet your tail. Why stick my neck out?"

Slocum's cool green eyes glittered. "That was interesting. The Kid was no killer. Wouldn't shoot in cold blood. He gave Cooper a fightin' chance. Gave him the odds, even. Because he let Cooper pull first."

Honey nodded slowly. "That's right, Slocum."

Slocum pulled out a cigarillo. "Maybe the Kid had a private grievance."

"If he did, Cooper didn't seem to know about it," said Honey.

Slocum looked thoughtful. "Maybe he knew, the moment before he croaked."

The stagecoach bumped along the trail in sight of a high line of cliffs. The sun was burning down hard. Not too far from the trail Slocum could see two deer

nervously drinking at a water hole. They suddenly lifted their heads and stiffened, then tore north at high speed as a puma lurched out of a nearby clump of cottonwoods, sprinting after them with a furious, clumsy gait. After a minute of hard pounding, the puma gave up the chase, panting, staring balefully after them, then turned to the water hole. He crouched down, lapped, rose to his feet, and stared north to where the deer scent still lingered.

Fowler suddenly spoke. "Hope we don't get any more excitement before we reach Abilene."

"Never know what's goin' to happen out here," Slocum said, smiling.

"Hope we don't run into Comanches," said Lucas.

"I hope so too," said Honey, her voice a bit sarcastic. "I didn't see any heroes here."

Lucas stared at her. "Heroes? Hard to be a hero with a gun pointing at you."

Honey's voice was cool. "It didn't stop Jared Cooper. He didn't button up his lip."

"Maybe Cooper would still be breathing if he'd kept his lip buttoned."

She ignored him, looking at Slocum. "You let that pipsqueak in a mask do what he wanted." She eyed him curiously. "Somehow you don't look like the sort of man who'd let that happen."

Slocum just smiled lazily.

Fowler spoke up. "That pipsqueak had the draw, Miss Honey. Sort of stupid to pull your gun in that setup."

She shrugged. "A good man would've done

something. We can't let drifting gunslingers do what they want. It ruins the territory."

Lucas was looking at her. "Easy for a woman to say. She doesn't have to put *her* life on the line."

Honey's lip curled. "Tell you the truth, Mr. Lucas, I was sorry I didn't have a gun."

Slocum leaned back in his seat. "You say your father knew Cooper?"

"Oh, yes. They were longtime acquaintances."

"Who's your father?"

"Bruce Braddock. We have the Bar-B, a spread a couple miles north of Cragg Creek."

Lucas turned sharply. "A spread she calls it. Miles and miles of land. I heard Braddock's the richest rancher in this territory." He stared at her. "Surprised your dad lets you travel the stage."

"Let's me?" Honey smiled. "Nobody *lets* me. I do as I please. It so happens I've been on a three-week visit to my Aunt Phyllis in Forth Worth."

Slocum liked the glint in her brown eyes. He liked the cut of her figure, too. Her blue shirt could hardly contain the swell of her bosom. She wore brown riding pants that clung nicely to well-packed buttocks. He had to laugh at her taste for heroics. Sounded like a girl who liked the excitement of gunfire.

He heard the yell of the stage driver as the horses slowed down. They had reached the main street of Cragg City, a line of weathered frame houses baking in the hot Texas sun.

The stagecoach depot was situated not far from the saloon, and when the stage came to a stop the sounds of the groaning springs and the hard breath-

ing of the tired horses perked up the quiet street. The saloon doors swung open, and two men came to the porch to watch the stage.

Casey helped Honey step down from the stage, and as he did, one of the two men, broad-shouldered and wearing a wide Stetson, strode across the dusty street.

Honey kissed him. "Hello, Dad."

He smiled at her, then stared at Casey. "Took your time getting here. I worried 'bout my little girl."

"Sorry, Mr. Braddock, but we got held up."

Braddock's face hardened. He stared at the green-eyed, lean, powerful stranger stepping out of the stage, followed by Lucas and Fowler. "Held up? What happened?" Braddock demanded.

"A masked gunslinger. A kid."

Slocum was startled at the cruel expression that came to Braddock's face. He had high cheekbones, reddish skin, fierce brown eyes, and a brush mustache. "Anyone get hurt? Where's Cooper?"

"Got hell shot outa him."

Braddock's eyes gleamed fiercely. "Dead? Jared dead? Can't believe it. Shot down in cold blood?"

"No, Dad," said Honey. "It was a draw."

Braddock showed his teeth, staring at the stagecoach riders. "You telling me that one boy in a mask stopped four grown men?"

"Yes, Daddy," Honey said. "Hardly any red-blooded men around anymore."

Braddock turned to Casey. "How much did he get?"

Casey shook his head. "He didn't stop for the money."

"Didn't stop for the money!" Braddock chewed his lip, then said, "S'pose you tell what happened. Quick-like."

Casey shrugged. "The robber stops us. He's a kid and wears a mask. Cooper don't like any of it. Says mean things. That gets the robber's goat. He tells us to throw our guns, but lets Cooper keep his. Then he insults Cooper, forces a draw, and pulls a fast gun. It's all up with Cooper." Casey looked puzzled. "I expected him to go for the money. But he didn't. He says, 'Drive on.'"

"He mighta gone for the money," said Honey, "but the gunfight stopped him."

"Mighty curious," said Braddock.

"Why?" asked Slocum.

Under thick brows, Braddock's fierce brown eyes studied the speaker. "Who are you?"

"Slocum's the name, John Slocum."

"Well, Mr. Slocum, it's not the first time this masked young buzzard pulled this stunt. Did it to Jim Welch and Charley Amis over in Silver Springs."

"Did what?"

"Did shootin', but not robbin'." Braddock's voice was harsh.

Honey said, "Maybe he's young, just startin' his crime career, Dad. He wants the money, but he gets caught up in a shoot-out, then runs away."

"You think that's it?" asked Braddock, turning to the others.

Lucas nodded. "I believe it, Mr. Braddock."

"Cooper was a friend of mine," Braddock said. "We're goin' to have to do something about this kid." He thoughtfully stroked his chin, then gazed at Slocum, at his cool green eyes, his square jaw, the lean, quick cut of him, the smooth handle of his Colt. To Braddock's experienced eye, Slocum looked like a fast gun. "You passin' through, mister, or staying in Cragg City?"

Slocum turned lazily. "Haven't given it much thought."

"I could use a quick hand. If you stay, I'd make it interestin' for you."

Honey looked at her father, then turned to Slocum, a flirtatious glint in her eye. "Think about it, Slocum. Lots of nice things out here."

Slocum couldn't help but smile. "Wouldn't be surprised."

Wheels creaked as a prancing white horse walked past pulling a buggy with two women, one gray-haired, the other young and striking looking. They nodded, and the men tipped their hats.

The buggy stopped at the general store, and the women stepped down. Slocum watched the young one, a pert figure in a gingham dress. Her hair was richly auburn and glowed in the sun. She walked toward the store, her head erect, her step graceful as a dancer. She paused at the doorway to look back at the stagecoach. Her eyes lingered on Slocum. He was captivated.

Honey's smile was wicked. "Yes, you might stick around, Slocum. We've got lots of nice things in Cragg City."

"No reason to hurry off," Slocum drawled. "One town's as good as another."

Slocum pushed through the batwing doors and walked in. It was a big saloon smelling of whiskey and smoke, with men standing at the bar or playing poker at the tables. Women in short bright dresses flounced among the men.

Slocum moved to the bar, almost unnoticed, and ordered whiskey from the barkeep, a red-faced, thick-featured man who slapped down the glass and bottle.

Slocum tossed off his drink and thought of the pert girl in the buggy who had given him an interesting look. Something about her had caught his fancy. A striking girl, the sort to easily fascinate a man. Even in that short time, he had picked up on her quality. It'd be interesting to discover who she was.

He poured another whiskey and noted Casey, the stage driver, come through the batwing doors, stomping his heavy boots. He took a spot near Slocum and said hello to some men nearby.

The bartender slapped whiskey and a glass in front of him. "Ridin' in late, Casey. What kept you?"

Casey gulped his whiskey. "We had a holdup, Jonesy."

The men nearby turned. Casey poured himself another drink, looked about, liking the attention. "You won't believe this. A kid, a sawed-off runt in a mask, stops us. Young, comin' outa nowhere. Gets into a brawl with Jared Cooper and shoots the hell outa him. Just like that."

There was a murmur of astonishment.

"That was it? Just one kid?" growled a burly, stubble-bearded man in soiled buckskins.

"Just him, Cokey," said the stagedriver. "Just him."

"Rob the stage, Casey?" asked another man.

"No, Hiram. He put a bullet in Cooper, then told us to drive on." Casey turned to Slocum. "That right, mister?"

The men at the bar looked curiously at the lean stranger with the cool green eyes.

"That's right, Casey," said Slocum.

Cokey, whose face was flushed with drink, examined Slocum with a jaundiced eye, then turned to Casey. "How many were you?" he asked.

"How many? Four. Honey Braddock was there."

Cokey's light blue eyes glittered. "You tellin' us a sawed-off kid shot Cooper? One little polecat, by himself? And a bunch of you let him do it? And Honey was there?"

Casey scowled. "He had the draw, Cokey. What could we do?"

Cokey shook his head in disbelief. He'd been guzzling and turned scornful eyes on Slocum, who coolly lit a cigarillo. He was thinking that Cokey was a drunk who'd easily go hostile, depending how liquor hit his mood.

Cokey kept chewing over what he'd just heard. "Lemme get this, Casey. Here comes this kid in a mask. He stops the wagon with four men. He shoots one of you. Takes off. And you let him?"

"I tole you, the polecat had a gun on us, Cokey."

Then Cokey, feeling his liquor, mocked Casey—

using a falsetto, almost feminine voice, he repeated, "The polecat had a gun on us."

It was comic, and the men at the bar couldn't help laughing. Slocum didn't smile.

Cokey noticed that but, encouraged by his audience, pushed it. "Here comes this sawed-off runt in a mask, and four big gunmen pee in their pants and watch him shoot down our friend Cooper." He stared at Slocum. "Sounds downright yellow to me."

Casey glanced nervously at Slocum.

Cokey noticed this and smirked. "Whatcha worried 'bout, Casey? A man who didn't pull his gun out there ain't goin' to do anything here."

The men at the bar turned to look at the stranger. If anyone had ever been challenged, this was it.

Slocum sighed. That was the trouble with saloons. There were always men who couldn't handle their whiskey—it made them vicious, itching to fight. The silence was clear. Any man who took such an insult wouldn't be considered a man; he laid himself open to contempt.

Slocum slowly turned. "You talking about me, Cokey?" His voice was mild, his face calm.

Cokey's eyes gleamed. "Reckon I must be, mister. You're the one I see."

Slocum dropped his cigarillo, stepped on it, and moved away from the bar. "And I see a man with a snoutful of whiskey and a loose mouth that could put him in trouble. Why don't you go somewhere and sleep it off?"

Cokey stared at Slocum, astounded at the man's

words—they were totally unexpected. Cokey had been ridin' high in front of the men, feeling safe, pickin' on a stranger whose gun was frozen in its holster, judging from the story of the stage. Now he found himself challenged by a man who showed no fear, who even looked dangerous. He glanced at the cowboys near him; they had backed off and were watching. He had boxed himself in, and there was no escape, he'd have to draw. And for what? For being a loudmouth whiskey-head. He had insulted this stranger, called him yellow. And the stranger hadn't taken the insult, which Cokey in alcoholic confidence had expected him to do. There was only one move he could make. He stepped away from the bar. "Mister, if there's sleepin', it's you who's goin' to do it."

There was sudden silence in the saloon, even at the poker games, as everyone turned to watch.

Cokey's hand went down to his holster, and he was pulling his gun when he saw a blur of movement and the fire from Slocum's hip. The bullet struck Cokey's hand and he yelped, dropping his gun and grabbing his hand. He stared at the blood and the crushed fingers, then looked in wonder at Slocum, with his cool green eyes. Cokey realized that, had he wanted to, the stranger could have drilled him through the heart. Cursing silently, Cokey wheeled and, holding his bleeding hand, barreled through the swinging doors.

Slocum slipped his gun into his holster, picked up his drink, and finished it.

Jones came over, smiling, and poured another

whiskey. "On the house, mister. That was fancy shootin'."

There was a pleased murmur from the men around, their eyes shining. Slocum couldn't help thinking that for men in the territory there were two entertainments—gunfights and women.

And it looked like the second was about to happen to Slocum as a pretty, well-rounded lady sidled up to him.

She was buxom, with hefty breasts and hips and a slender waist, very suited to his taste. Her eyes were alert, her cheekbones high, her mouth full. A surprising looker for such a place.

"I'm Rosebud, and I've got a thirst."

He grinned. "I'm Slocum, and I've got a hunger." He poured a drink. "For your thirst."

She looked at him through slitted eyes and ran a hand over her breast and hip. "For your hunger."

He grinned, and they both drank.

"I like the way you pulled your gun," she said.

"Nice to hear."

Her voice was low. "Cokey's a bully—it comes out with the whiskey."

Slocum nodded. "Yeah, whiskey brings a lot out in a man."

A slow smile twisted her full lips. "You got a wicked way of talkin', Slocum."

He lit a cigarillo and smiled. "Talk wicked to a wicked woman."

"Seems I saw you in town before."

He nodded. "I was here. Brought my horse in lame. Left him at the livery and took the stage to Clay Corners to see an old friend." He thought of

Cole, who used to ride with him in the Quantrill days. It had been a good visit, with drinks and remembering. Slocum smiled grimly. "On the way back in the stage we lost Jared Cooper to a fast-drawing boy."

"Jared Cooper." Her voice was dry. "Another prize specimen. He won't be missed."

"You weren't fond of him?"

"Nearest thing to a buzzard in human form," she said.

It fit in with his own opinion of the man. Slocum smoked silently.

"Where you from, Slocum? I hear a down-home accent."

"Calhoun County, Georgia."

She smiled. "I'm a Dixie girl myself. Carolina. What brought you out to Cragg City?"

"Just driftin'," he said, looking away. He was looking at the cardplayers nearby, but seeing his old plantation. The ancestral home of the Slocums for generations until that carpetbagger judge came to claim it. The land where he'd been born, Slocum's blood and sweat had nourished the ground, and here came this carpetbagger to claim it: spoils of war.

In his time, Slocum had known rage, but none matched the fury that swept over him that moment. The carpetbagger was a judge, but he was struck just as dead as if he'd been a thief. Yes, in the end the judge got the land, but only six feet deep of it. Afterward Slocum ran for the territories, condemned to drifting.

Caught in memory, he lifted his glass, feeling echoes of the rage.

Rosebud had picked up his tension. She had a way of handling such feelings in men. "What kind of hunger were you talkin' about before, Slocum?"

It brought him back, and he looked at her. "Woman hunger."

She leaned to him, her full breast touching his arm, and whispered, "I've got a nice bed upstairs."

He followed her, and the movement of her buttocks put the craving in his groin.

The room was plain, with a pine bed, a square table on which stood a whiskey bottle and two glasses, a straight-back chair, and a chest with a water basin and an enamel pitcher. The window looked down on the dusty main street, and he could see the hotel and the bank. He turned to watch her pull her dress off, revealing her plump breasts, small waist, full hips, and her gartered stockings. The pink nipples of her breasts were small. He stood there looking at her.

She glanced at him, a small smile at the corner of her lips. "Is that what you're goin' to do, stand and look?"

He laughed and stripped, and the excitement of his flesh was boldly visible. She gazed at him with appreciation. "Nothing so nice to an interested woman than the sight of a strappin', healthy male in heat."

He laughed. "And nothing so nice to a man in heat than a fine-looking filly with the right curves."

She came close, and his hands went over her soft

skin, the swell of her breasts. He bent and put his tongue to a nipple, while his hand moved to her secret places. They played like this for a time, and her breath came faster. She bent to his body, her lips moving over it, exploring boldly. He felt strong pulsations of pleasure. Finally they moved to the bed. Her thighs came apart to receive him, and he felt her moist warmth. He began slow moves, and her body picked up his rhythm. They went on like this, then her hips began to writhe and he felt the gathering tension. His movements became more urgent, and he held her tight until the explosive surge. She held him and moaned softly.

After they dressed, she poured two glasses of whiskey and they drank. She gazed at him. "You're a good man with a gun, Slocum. In more ways than one."

He smiled. "Always nice to be appreciated."

They sat in silence, and from the window he could see a crimson sky as the sun moved to the horizon. He sipped his drink. "I reckon you know Braddock."

She nodded. "Braddock? Everyone knows him. Why?"

"Wants me to work for him."

She shrugged. "Well, Braddock's the big gun round here. Lots of land, lots of money, lots of muscle." She smiled wickedly. "His daughter, Honey, is a brazen thing. She could put me outa business if she wanted."

He laughed.

She stared. "What's the laugh?"

"I believe you." Slocum looked out the window.

"How'd Braddock get so rich? Buying cattle?"

"He came here rich. Had money from the beginning. Bought the Prescott spread, lock, stock, and barrel."

"Big cattle stock?"

"Big everything. Owns the Cragg City Bank, too." She shook her head. "So he wants you to work for him. Gun work, probably."

He looked at her.

"He likes to have smart guns around," she said.

"Why?"

"He's got a lot to protect, is why."

Slocum grinned and put money on the chest. "You're very savvy, Rosebud."

"It's the business I'm in." She picked up the money and slipped it into her gartered stocking. "You must come back again."

As Slocum went down the stairs, he couldn't help but congratulate himself. If you wanted to pick up the dirt in a town, the quickest way was through a smart saloon lady. The mattress was a place where the most astonishing secrets got revealed.

He walked out to the street and toward the hotel. The setting sun was paving the distant cliffs with gold.

The painted sign on the wooden front said "Cragg City Hotel," and as Slocum walked into the lobby to check in, he thought about Braddock, of Honey, of the girl in the buggy, of the Masked Kid.

Cragg City, he figured, had interesting possibilities.

2

The sun was rising in a light blue sky when Slocum walked from the hotel to the livery, where he'd left the roan. The horse had gone lame the first time Slocum had come to Cragg City, and he had decided to continue on the stagecoach to Clay Corners for his visit with Cole.

In the days when bluecoat bullets cracked around them, Cole had been a dependable sidekick. It had been a nice visit, and over drinks they had raked up old times. Cole and he had done plenty of damage to the other side in those days.

By now the roan should be back in shape, Slocum thought as he walked into the livery where Turner, the smith, was holding his hammer. He had a broad face, a muscular chest, and thick, hairy forearms. Slocum saw the roan in his stall, his big black eyes glittering, his ears high. As Slocum

walked close, he realized again his deep feelings for the horse. He stroked the velvet flank; the roan whinnied and nudged him roughly, as if to tell how grieved he'd been to be abandoned by his master. Slocum looked at the left foreleg. It looked good.

"How's he moving, Turner?"

"Moves like silk, Mr. Slocum. A great horse."

Slocum nodded. He couldn't count the times the roan had taken him out of trouble. He stroked the flank, and the thought of fine bloodlines put him in mind of the girl in the buggy.

"By the way, Turner, a buggy with two ladies came to town."

There was no need to go further. Turner was grinning. "You're talking of Mrs. Bakely and her niece, Jane. They have a small spread out near the butte. Beautiful girl, Jane. Sort of mysterious. Moved in with her aunt six months ago. Don't know where she came from—maybe Phoenix. She's pretty as a picture but keeps her distance. None of the young sparks can get a rise out of her." He smiled slyly. "Noticed her? Well, she got's something."

Slocum was running his hand over the roan. "She's got what this horse has."

Turner grinned widely. "And what's that?"

Slocum looked at him. "Don't you know? Breeding. Spirit."

The smith stroked his chin. "All I know is horses, Mr. Slocum. I'll leave the other to you."

•   •   •

He was walking from the livery to Laura's Cafe, when he heard the deep voice.

"Slocum."

The voice was familiar, and he turned. There stood Bill Sykes in his broad black hat, yellow vest, and holstered gun over his tight Levi's. The piercing black eyes stared out of his lean, high-cheeked face. Slocum felt a flicker of anger, remembering Sykes.

"Well, Sykes. I thought you were working the Panhandle."

Sykes didn't smile. He never smiled that Slocum remembered. A hard-eyed vicious bounty hunter who worked the Panhandle with an uncanny talent for getting his man and bringing him in dead.

"Who you out to kill this time, Sykes?"

Sykes's thin lips twisted. He might joke but never smiled. "C'mon, Slocum, you're not still thinkin' 'bout Caine?"

"Not easy to forget Caine," Slocum said. Two months ago, on a street in Sante Fe, working as a bounty hunter, Slocum had cornered his quarry, Dave Caine.

"They want you back in Tucson," he had told Caine, a square-faced, honest-looking cowboy, who had shot a man over a woman.

Caine looked grimly at Slocum, whom he had heard about, and figured he might get a fair shake if he surrendered to Slocum.

But there was three hundred dollars posted on him, and Sykes, also a bounty man hunting Caine, suddenly fired from the doorway of the saloon. Caine had dropped to the dust in the street and

stared up at Slocum. "I'm kilt," he said slowly. "And I'm innocent." Then he died.

Slocum in a rage had turned to Sykes, who, still holding his gun, had come forward.

"Why the hell did you do that?" Slocum was white-faced.

Sykes looked grim. "Caine was a wanted outlaw, that's why."

Slocum's voice was icy. "He was wanted for *trial*, not for *burying*."

Bill Sykes glanced at the dead man, his voice cool. "He was posted an outlaw, and a dead outlaw is less trouble to bring in." Sykes watched Slocum carefully. "Don't try anything foolish. Men like us ought not to fight over men like him. Caine is better off dead."

Slocum looked at Caine, his eyes staring empty at the sky. He had killed a man over a woman, but he might have shot in self-defense—there was no way to know until witnesses talked up.

"We got a jury in Tucson to say who's better off dead, Sykes. It ain't your job."

There was a bad moment. Bill Sykes, a fabled gun, feared no man, and didn't take a challenge lightly. He knew Slocum and didn't fear him, but at the moment, he saw no personal profit in a shoot-out.

"Okay, Slocum, let's say I made a mistake. But it's done. Can't bring a dead man back. Let's have a drink and forget it. If you won't share the bounty money, it's all right. I won't claim it." Sykes's face was grim. "Of course, you didn't face a draw. I spared you that. So, if you'd like to share . . ."

Slocum scowled. "Sykes, you won't get a dime of that bounty money. And I won't either. Though I'm bringing Caine back, I'm not claimin' him."

For a moment Sykes's brown eyes glittered. "That's not smart, Slocum." He didn't like it. But he decided not to do anything.

Sykes, however, had a good memory for such things.

Looking at Sykes now in Cragg City, Slocum remembered it all.

"So what are you here for, Sykes?"

"I got business with Braddock." Sykes's piercing gaze stayed on Slocum. "Reckon that's what you're here for. Braddock is collecting smart guns."

Slocum rubbed his chin. That clinched it, he was thinking. If Braddock wanted Sykes, the job had to be rotten. Slocum couldn't see himself hitched alongside a sleazy gunslinger like Sykes.

"Is that what you're here for, Slocum?"

"No. That's not why." Slocum looked down the street and saw Jane Bakely come out of the bank and walk toward the cafe. Slocum watched her, admiring her light, graceful walk.

"So that's what you're here for?" Sykes's thin lips twisted, the only way he smiled.

Slocum shrugged, and remembering he'd had no breakfast, started for the cafe.

Laura's Cafe was large and comfortable, with a double lineup of square tables and a door opening on the kitchen. An old-timer with faded blue eyes was eating at a table at the far end. Jane Bakely sat near

the window talking to a stout, smiling woman wearing an apron.

She excused herself from Jane and came toward Slocum with a broad grin. "Hi. I'm Laura."

"Slocum. John Slocum."

"Mr. Slocum, you look like a man with a healthy appetite."

Slocum glanced at the beautiful girl sitting alone with her coffee and biscuits.

Laura picked it up. "I'm talking about food, Mr. Slocum."

He smiled. "It's nourishing to look at some women. I'll have eggs, bacon, biscuits, and coffee."

Laura nodded. "Fix it right up. You just passin' through or stayin'?"

"Thinking about it." He smiled dryly. "Mr. Braddock wants a good hand."

Jane Bakely had been sipping coffee and gazing out the window. Now she turned, and Slocum felt her scrutinizing him.

"Mr. Braddock?" said Laura. "Well, he's got the money to hire anyone." She walked toward her kitchen.

Slocum turned toward Jane Bakely. Her blue eyes were on him, and, to his mild surprise, she didn't seem disconcerted by his own stare. She was one hell of a looker, he thought, with the fine bones of her face, chiseled nose, wide mouth, and crown of auburn hair.

"Something on your mind, miss?"

"Were you thinking of working for Braddock?" Her voice was almost mellow.

"That interest you, miss?"

"Somewhat," she said. "I'm not one to advise you, but you're a stranger. I'd steer clear of Braddock and his men."

He reached into his shirt pocket for a cigarillo. "Why's that, Miss...?"

"Jane Bakely. You look honest. You ought not to throw in with Braddock."

His eyebrows went up. "Nobody's called him a horse thief. Maybe you've got a personal beef?"

"As I said, I'd steer clear of Braddock."

"But you haven't given a reason, Miss Jane."

She hesitated, as if she was ready to stop talking, but then said, "Braddock seems to be a dangerous man to work for."

"Dangerous?" he smiled.

"A lot of dyin' around him," she said.

Slocum looked thoughtful. "He's bad luck, is that it?"

"I've nothing more to say."

Just then Laura brought out his eggs and bacon, and Slocum turned to it with gusto.

Jane Bakely finished her coffee and started toward the door, passing Slocum.

"Whyn't you sit here, Miss Jane," Slocum said politely. "We might talk more about Braddock."

"Nothing more to say." Her intense blue eyes looked at him directly, and she turned toward the door.

At that moment two burly men, with flat black hats and the look of gunslingers came in. The first man, with mocking eyes, for reasons of his own bumped Jane. And Jane, who had been looking at

Slocum, was caught off balance. She went to the floor.

To Slocum, the gunslinger's move had been deliberate, and he stood looking at her, making no effort to help her up.

"Clumsy filly," he said. "You should watch where you're goin'." He seemed to give his words special meaning.

Slocum's face was flushed. He leaned down to help Jane to her feet, then turned to the gunslinger, who was watching with cool, shiny black eyes. He was either a lowdown skunk or had something against Jane Bakely.

"Not much of a gentleman," Slocum said.

"Not much. What about it?" His voice was low, harsh.

Slocum's right fist, with the power of his shoulder muscles behind it, shot out, hitting the man's jaw. He was flung back against his thick-featured sidekick and sank to the floor, stunned.

His sidekick's face twisted ugly, and he bent to the fallen man, stopped, and started to bring his gun out, but Slocum brought the edge of his hand down hard on his wrist and the gun skittered to the floor. Slocum kicked it. The gunman held his wrist, glared viciously at Slocum, then bent to the fallen man.

"Frank, you all right?"

Frank, his eyes glazed, gritted his teeth. "Yeah. Yeah, Willie." He shook his head, as if trying to clear it, and got slowly to one knee, staring at Slocum. "Next time we meet, mister, pull your gun."

Slocum said nothing, but followed Jane, who had

gone out of the cafe. She walked easy and slowed down for him.

"I've met rotten buzzards in my time," Slocum drawled, "but never one to trip a lady. Why'd he do it?"

"Maybe he has reasons," she said.

"Like what?"

"I'm no friend to Braddock, as you have heard. These men work for him." She looked at Slocum, her face cool. "I appreciate your help, Mr. Slocum. But I fear you've put yourself in danger."

"What danger?"

"This Frank, he's a gunfighter. A Braddock man. He's shot two men in fights at the saloon." She studied him. "It might be better, Mr. Slocum, to keep riding, to leave town."

He smiled. "I don't leave a town until I'm ready. And I'm not ready."

She had reached her buggy and climbed up. She picked up the reins, looked down at Slocum, her cool, lovely face measuring him. "Perhaps you'd like a home-cooked supper, Mr. Slocum? In that case, some early evening you might ride out to the Bakely ranch. It's right next to the Braddock spread. Braddock has miles of land, but we've got the stream." Her blue eyes glittered. "You see, Mr. Slocum, Mr. Braddock envies our land, he wants it. It's got water. Come and see us."

She flicked the reins, and the white horse began to prance forward.

He watched her, admiring the way the sun struck her auburn hair.

3

Slocum walked down the street, pausing to look at
the bank. There was a hard-faced guard in a blue
jacket standing at the door. The bank, Slocum remembered, also belonged to Braddock. Why was it,
Slocum wondered, that big landowners also owned
banks? Probably it had to do with power, because if
you owned the bank, you could dominate the land
and the folks. And Braddock looked like a man
with a taste for that kind of stuff.

Slocum thought with a small smile of Braddock's
offer of a job. If he worked for Braddock, he'd get
orders to do ornery gun jobs alongside polecats like
Sykes. Honey, too, wanted him at the ranch; she
was one sexy filly, who'd like to play games. He
might talk to Braddock, just to hear his pitch.

By this time, Slocum had reached the livery. He

had decided to take the roan out, put him through paces, to see if the lameness was gone.

Turner was busy with a customer, so Slocum waved, saddled the roan, and walked him out to the street, watching him move with the grace of a thoroughbred. It felt good to be in the saddle, to feel the strength of the horse, just walking him down the street. Out of town, he put him in a gentle canter. There was no faltering, no favoring of the lame foreleg.

They headed west toward the great spread of cliffs towering under a dazzling blue sky. He followed the trail until he reached a flat spread of land and put the roan into a fast run, watching for the slightest falter, but the horse moved like silk. Slocum, tuned to the spirit of the roan, sensed its joy in movement.

He pulled the reins to give the horse a breather and looked at the land with pleasure. It was handsome country, with rich grass, leafy cottonwoods, swale and thistle, some boulders, and in the distance, the jagged line of majestic mountains stretching west. A lone eagle soared high in the sky, riding the wind, and a buzzard lazily circled an unseen carcass below.

Slocum rode another hour, moving into high ground. He found a niche at a boulder where he camped, made coffee, and ate a couple of strips of jerky. It was a high rise of land, and from the ledge he could see the trail below and the long view to the west. The coffee gave him a nice lift, and an exaltation came to him. He felt free in a vast, beautiful, open country.

It was then that he spotted the stagecoach from Green River headed for Cragg City. There was no shotgun rider alongside the driver, no money being transported, and the stage, perhaps ahead of it schedule, moved at a leisurely pace.

Slocum watched it idly, sipping coffee, and it was about a thousand yards from his point of vision when he heard the shot.

A rider had appeared from behind a boulder, holding a gun. Slocum, in astonishment, realized it was again the Masked Kid wearing black. His shot had been a warning to the driver to slow down. The stage rolled to a stop, and the Kid, staying behind a low crag, shouted orders at the passengers.

They came out—two women, a dude in eastern clothes, and a husky rancher wearing a wide Stetson, a black vest, and holstering a gun.

The Kid ordered the driver to throw down his rifle and the passengers to move to the side. To Slocum, he seemed to be doing what he'd done with the other stagecoach, concentrating on one man, allowing him to keep his gun.

Slocum, too far to hear, watched, fascinated. The Kid, still holding his gun, moved in front of the husky man. They talked while the others watched. Whatever the Kid said seemed to jolt the man in the Stetson; he moved restlessly and looked around, as if for a place to run.

The Masked Kid stepped back a few paces and put his gun in its holster.

Slocum watched, rooted to the spot. It looked like a replay of the draw incident in his stagecoach.

A sudden movement as both men went for their

guns. One fired, and the man in the Stetson staggered, bent over in pain, and went slowly down.

The Kid watched him, as if the death meant a lot. Finally he turned to the others and gave them an order. They piled in the stage, and the driver took off, leaving in a flurry of dust. The Kid watched them, looked down at the dead man, then walked to the saddle of his horse and pulled out a shovel.

Slocum shook his head. What did you do in a situation like this? The Kid had done no crime. He didn't steal. He gave his opponent a fair draw.

But why the hell was he doing this?

The afternoon sun was a blaze of yellow in the summer sky, and Slocum, riding southwest toward the Braddock ranch, paused several times in the shade of a cottonwood to cool down. Sweat gleamed off the coat of the roan. When finally Slocum found a waterhole, not too far from the Braddock spread, he stopped to let the roan drink.

He had just bent toward the water when he heard the bark of a rifle bounce off the crags as the bullet nicked his arm. He dropped flat, as if hit bad, and crawled toward the nearby boulder. Two more bullets kicked the dirt around him.

Crouched behind the small boulder, he looked at the wound. It was very slight, just the edge of his upper arm; the blood leaked slowly. He tied a kerchief around his arm to stop the bleeding. After a few deep breaths, he cautiously peered at a high ledge, where he caught the glitter of sun on metal.

He waited, feeling the sweat, wondering who in hell was trying to ambush him. Again he peered

out. No sign of movement. He studied the surrounding terrain. There was a bigger boulder nearby that offered better cover. Should he move?

He peered at the ledge, ready to duck. Nothing. He waited, put his pistol under his Stetson, and raised it above the boulder to draw fire. Nothing. Had the gunman, whoever the hell he was, sneaked off? He needed just to retreat behind the hill of rocks to where he had tethered his horse below.

Slocum started a cautious climb, staying down, sticking to cover, though he believed the sneak gunman had departed after firing. It was slow going, but finally he reached the ledge. There were prints that went toward the bottom of the rocks. Slocum studied the boot prints, then went back to his roan and rode around the hill to pick up the tracks of the gunman's horse: not an unshod pony, not an Apache.

He followed the tracks, which went west, and as the sun crept down, to his surprise, he smelled smoke. This sneaky gunman couldn't be too bright, for he'd stopped to camp.

Slocum tethered the roan and moved soundlessly toward the smoke. Finally he came in sight of a man crouched at a fire, sipping coffee from a tin cup. Slocum stared at him in surprise. It was a familiar face—Frank's sidekick, the man called Willie. A gunman, all right, but why'd he try ambush, and why stop here, as if he didn't expect to be tracked down? But this was Willie's terrain, near the Braddock land.

Slocum, his jaw hard, walked softly toward the gunman, who seemed lost in thought.

"Hello, Willie."

Willie looked up, astonished to see the lean, square-faced cowboy in the Stetson, staring at him with piercing green eyes. The main thing was, his gun was in his holster.

"What the hell," Willie said.

"You can't be surprised," Slocum said.

Willie took his time, thinking. Slocum didn't hold a gun, didn't look threatening. "Should I be?"

"Been here long?" Slocum asked.

"Long enough," Willie said. He had a brutal face, and his lips were wreathed in a half smile. He stood up easily.

"You aimin' to leave?" Slocum asked.

"Got any objections?"

"Somebody tried to bushwhack me back there."

Willie's eyes gleamed, but his lips kept their half smile.

"Yeah? Why would they do that?"

Slocum smiled grimly. "It's a good question. Why'd *you* do it, Willie?"

Willie's smile widened. "Me? Is that a joke?"

"I followed your tracks, mister. You must be stupid to stop like this." Slocum stared hard. "Got nothing to fear, is that it?"

Willie's glance was contemptuous. "Nothin' much." His hand was near his gun. He had done his share of killing, and he was confident of his draw. "I'll tell you, mister. It wasn't stupid to stop. Maybe I been expectin' you. I didn't like the way you hit my sidekick, Frank, the other day. Didn't like the way you hit me. I promised myself to get a bullet in you for that."

He stroked his bony chin with his left hand. "When I spotted you at the water hole, I didn't think you deserved a shoot-out. Figured it was a good time to pay you off. To tell the truth, I thought I hit you, that you were bleeding to death behind your rock." His grin widened.

Slocum stared at him. "Nothing I despise more than a low-down, sneakin' bushwhacker. Why don't you pull your gun."

Willie laughed. He took two slow steps back. "It's goin' to be nice to kill you twice, mister. I'll see you get a real burying this time." His hand went for his gun as he talked.

Slocum seemed to watch him for a split second, then he moved. His gun spit fire, knocking Willie back, the wound in his chest pouring blood. He staggered, his face frozen with the shock that he'd lost and death had entered his body. He fell on his back, and his eyes slowly became dull.

Slocum stared down at him. Then something touched the edge of his mind and he turned to look up.

There, near the edge of a high, out-thrusting crag, someone on a horse was looking down at him. He looked like a sculptured monument.

Slocum bit his lip. It was the Masked Kid, in black. He turned his horse and moved down out of sight.

The roan jogged on, and Slocum looked down from a high rise, at the stretch of land below. To the east was the huge Braddock spread, with corrals of horses and great herds of grazing cattle; west of it

lay the Bakely ranch—a buggy, a couple of horses, a few chickens and cows. But a stream twisted through the land.

Slocum looked back to the Braddock land, where men were gathered around the corral, watching a cowboy trying to break a bronc. As Slocum moved closer, he recognized among the watchers leaning on the corral fence the broad-shouldered Braddock and the sinewy Sykes. He spotted Honey on the other side of the corral.

As Slocum closed in, one of the men noticed him and said something, and the men glanced around. Braddock looked pleased, though he went back to watching the bucking bronc. The bronc took another thirty seconds to heave the rider, who went off in a sickening arc through the air. After dumping his rider, the bronc kept kicking wildly.

The cowboys laughed loudly, a couple slapping their thighs. Honey also smiled from her perch on the fence. The bronc, aware finally that he'd dumped the hated rider, circled the corral, as if on parade, then stood quiet, as if daring another two-footed idiot to try him.

Slocum swung off the roan and walked toward the corral.

Braddock gave him a broad smile and put out his hand. "Glad to see you, Slocum. You here to join up?"

"I'm here to talk about it."

Braddock's fierce brown eyes gleamed, then he smiled. "Sure. Sure, Slocum." He turned to the man on his right. "This is Sykes, one of my best boys."

Slocum looked at the piercing black eyes, the high-cheeked, lean, unsmiling face.

Sykes's voice was cool. "I know Slocum."

Surprised, Braddock glanced from one to the other, sensing something. "Yeah? How do you know each other?"

Slocum casually pulled a cigarillo from his shirt pocket.

Sykes, with a twist of his lips, spoke. "We were on a bounty hunt for the same man in Waco."

Braddock found that interesting and grinned. "Yeah? And who got him?"

Sykes waited for Slocum, but he seemed busy striking a lucifer. "Well," he drawled, "Slocum trapped him. But I shot him."

This too pleased Braddock. "That's good. Teamwork, the kind I want here." He rubbed his hands for a moment. "So you shared the bounty."

"There was no bounty," Slocum said. "The man called Caine was innocent, they found out later. He never should have been shot."

Braddock frowned.

Sykes looked grim. "They posted Caine an outlaw. He killed a man. That was enough for me."

Braddock fingered his brush mustache, thinking. He stared at Slocum. "Just between us, mister, I like a man who shoots first and asks later. You get to see a lot of sunsets that way. Once in a while you make a mistake." He grinned broadly. "But nobody's perfect."

Just then an intrepid cowboy climbed the corral fence and started toward the bronc. A cheer went up from the watching men. The ears of the bronc

stiffened as it watched the cowboy approach, but that was its only movement.

Honey Braddock was perched on the other side of the fence, surrounded by three husky cowboys. She caught Slocum's eye and smiled broadly. The cowboys stared at Slocum, but he had turned to Braddock.

The broad-shouldered rancher put his hand on Slocum's arm. "I can tell that a man like you, Slocum, with Sykes here and a couple of other picked guns, could take good care of my troubles. I'd like to have you with me. I'll pay plenty, but we'll talk about it later. Just now it ought to be fun to see who's gonna break down that bronc." He glanced at the rangy cowboy edging carefully toward the bronc.

Slocum smiled too as he looked at the bronc, a mare, who showed no emotion as her black eyes followed the cowboy.

Everyone watched with fierce interest, Slocum noticed. There was something in the contest of man and brute that held primitive fascination and went back to the beginnings, when man set out to dominate his world.

The rangy cowboy moved warily around the horse and suddenly slipped over her back.

There was no movement.

The bronc stood as if made of stone.

Everyone laughed.

The cowboy reached for his hat and slapped it with a flourish. That did it. The bronc came to sudden life and within seconds turned into a snarling, twisting, kicking demon of fury.

The cowboy hung on valiantly, then turned into a bouncing rag doll and was flung through the air, landing on his back. He lay, stunned for a moment, then, aware that the bronc was still in a kicking frenzy, he staggered to the safety of the fence.

The onlookers roared with delight. Slocum laughed too: there was joy in watching an animal whose spirit fought off bondage. It was fun, Slocum believed, because resistance was interesting. But in the end, man was expected to win.

Honey, sitting on the fence, enjoyed the spectacle hugely, because, Slocum suspected, it was a mare that was humiliating the male rider. Women like her liked that.

Braddock turned to him. "Ain't nobody gonna ride that horse now. Let's go over to the house and have a couple of drinks."

Slocum glanced at Honey, and she waved at him.

He followed Braddock and Sykes into the big ranch house, where, in the living room, they were served fine whiskey by a white-coated servant named Lopez.

They downed the drinks and the refills.

"I've got troubles," Braddock began. "Rustlers. There's a gang up north that keeps pickin' off my strays, and some of my best longhorns. And there's some wild bucks, Apaches, who raid my northwest range. We've got to run these thieving dogs to ground."

Braddock paused, and his brown eyes took on a ferocious glitter. "Last but not least, there's that robbin' coyote who keeps stoppin' the stage and shootin' folks. Got to nail him, too." He lifted his

glass. "Just between us, I'd like to put him on the top of our killin' list."

"Why?" Slocum asked.

Braddock turned sharply. "Why? Because he's killin' innocent men. The others are just thievin', but this Masked Kid is killin'."

"He's not shooting in cold blood, though," Slocum said.

Braddock's face hardened. "What do you mean?"

"He stops the stage, but he doesn't steal. He gives one man a fighting chance. It's a draw. I've seen it. Twice."

"Twice?" Sykes looked at him. "Where was the second time?"

"The Green River stage. I was in the hills. Saw it all."

Sykes nodded and turned to Braddock. "In a way of talkin', the kid's not doin' a crime, if it's a fair draw."

Braddock's face flushed. "But he's fast. And he's *forcin'* the draw. It's like murder." Braddock scowled at Slocum. "S'pose Billy the Kid forced you to draw. That'd be murder, wouldn't it?"

Slocum smiled. "We'll never know. He's dead."

Braddock didn't see the joke. "Who the hell is this kid? What gives him the right to stop stages and shoot folks? No, it's got to stop. He's shot Jared Cooper and Jim Welch and Charley Amis. Wonder who he shot on the Green River stage. We know these men. Decent law-abiding citizens. What's he after, this masked kid, anyway?" He shrugged.

"Hell. Whatever it is, we've got to mow him down. That's what I want you boys to do."

Braddock's fierce eyes scowled at Slocum. "I'm paying big money. Two hundred dollars a month and a special bonus for the man who puts the kid six feet under. What do you say, Slocum?"

Slocum rubbed his chin. "I don't know. I had in mind something else. Give me a day to think about it."

Sykes looked at his fingernails.

Braddock's face showed disappointment. "Okay. It's good money. You can't do better anywhere. Come in with us, Slocum. You won't be sorry."

The roan trotted easily, a pace he could hold forever, it seemed to Slocum. He was two miles out of the Braddock ranch, and the sun hung low in the sky, a mammoth orange. Slocum liked this time of day, when the fiery light gilded the seared stone of the crags and peaks. He felt the beauty of nature as he rode, and he took pleasure in it.

Then his mind went back to Braddock. The cattleman was paying good money, and most men would grab the offer. But Slocum didn't cotton to men like Braddock. Land sharks, he thought them. According to Jane Bakely, he craved her skimpy land because of its water. Also, Braddock had men around like Sykes, a bounty buzzard who'd kill first and ask questions later. Well, you needed buzzards like Sykes to clear out rustlers, yes. But what did you make of Braddock's big fuss about the Masked Kid? He seemed more hot and bothered about the Kid, who was doing nothing to him, than about the

rustlers who were stealing his stock. That was strange. For Slocum, the Kid was a riddle. He didn't rob, he was polite, and he didn't shoot in cold blood. It was always a draw. He put his own life on the line, doing that. The mystery of the Kid gnawed at Slocum. He had a style, the Kid did, almost elegant, the way he handled himself, the way he went about his business. What business? Was it random killing or done with a purpose? Who knew? Who was being killed? And why?

And was it his own business? Slocum wondered. In the territories, men shot each other for the wrong word, even for the wrong look. And if you got involved in every piece of injustice, you wouldn't last a day. It was smart to mind your own business, to keep your gun clean and be ready to defend your life. You needed to be faster than the other guy, because to come in a split-second behind him meant death.

Slocum took a deep breath, noticing the land with its thickets of staghorn sumac, steep slopes covered with fern and lichen. Always alert at any site that presented ambush, he heard a soft sound, and his hand went to his gun.

"Don't shoot, Slocum," Honey said.

She came out in full view from behind some piled-up crags. She was smiling. "It took you long enough to get here." She had started out before him, racing on the trail to reach this spot.

"No hurry," he said.

"No, I s'pose not. Don't see you as a man who'd hurry for anything." She leaned her body gracefully against a boulder.

He swung off his horse and pulled out his canteen. She watched him with a half smile. She wore a light blue shirt, tightly tailored, that showed her abundant breasts. She had a small waist and full hips. A womanly woman, he thought.

"Move fast enough when I have to," he said.

"I'm sure you do, Slocum. That's why Dad wants you." She smiled serenely. "And what Dad wants, he usually gets." Leaning against the boulder the way she did threw her breasts forward.

"Like father, like daughter," she said, then sat down on a low stone slab next to the boulder.

"But he gets what he wants by buying it."

"What's wrong with that?" she demanded. "That's how it works."

He shrugged. "Some things can't be bought."

She shook her head. "Everyone has a price, Slocum." Her blue eyes fixed on him. "Even you."

He looked at her. "And what's yours?"

She looked off. "Dad says you haven't made up your mind to join us. What's stopped you?"

"I'm thinking about it." He pulled a cigarillo from his shirt pocket and lit it.

"What's to think about? Rustlers stealing? Gotta stop that or the thieves will take over. We can't let that happen."

There's more than one way to thieve, Slocum thought, wondering how Braddock had got all his stock, all his land. In Slocum's experience most land barons in the territories got it by grabbing. Well, it was a raw country, and you got your piece of it any way you could, and the quick way was a bullet in your opponent.

She watched him. "So what will it take to bring you to the Braddocks?" She pushed her sizable breasts at him.

"I'm thinking about it."

"Dad has offered you good money. It hasn't tempted you. Maybe you need gentle persuasion."

She stood up and moved close to him. It was easy to understand why she was called Honey. A pretty face, with dark glowing eyes, thrusting breasts that now teased against him.

He stared into the depths of her eyes, which glittered with the low-banked fire of desire. He felt his own body tingle.

"Why don't I try to persuade you," she said, moving against him, and he felt her body. She pressed her mouth to his, and her hands went down boldly over him. What she felt made her sigh with pleasure. She pulled at him, and they went down between a shelter of rocks onto the grass. It took just moments to strip. Nude, she was all woman, with swollen breasts, a flat stomach, shapely legs, and full hips. His hands moved over her body, over the smooth breasts, the hard pink nipples, her smooth stomach, her buttocks.

He put his tongue to her nipple, and his fingers explored the pouting lips between her thighs. She groaned; she was one ready lady. Soon she turned on him, her mouth exploring his body. She was very good, and brought him so high it almost finished him. He pushed her back. Her legs came apart and he eased into her. She squirmed and moaned, and he took hold of her smooth buttocks and drove into her. She caught his rhythm and made soft screech-

ing sounds. Then she grabbed his waist and flung against him as all sorts of things happened to her body. He felt his own surge and exploded. She kept groaning and writhing.

After they had dressed, she turned to him with a confident smile. "Now will you join us, Slocum?"

"You're very persuasive," he said. She was a sexy lady, but he didn't make decisions because of a quick screw on the trail.

She looked astonished. "Does that mean yes or no?"

"We'll see." His voice was pleasant.

Honey's wide mouth tightened. "I hope I didn't waste my lovin'," she rasped.

He gazed at her innocently. "Why, Honey, I can't believe you did it for anything but your own pleasure."

She bit her lips with small white teeth. "All right, Slocum. It was a pleasure. You're a real man. So think about it and come in with us. Dad will like it. And I'll be happy to show my appreciation."

Later, as Slocum rode toward town, he couldn't help but think that father and daughter came off the same tree. Braddock got what he wanted with the gun, and Honey with her body. But Slocum, who had lost his own land in Georgia because of a tricky carpetbagger, found himself already in sympathy with Jane Bakely. He'd ride out there tomorrow for that home-cooked dinner she'd promised.

4

Next day, he rode out to the Bakely land. The sun was low by then, heading down toward the peaks of the western spread of stone. The land smelled summer sweet, and he saw a coyote scrambling after a rabbit, a buzzard flying in a lazy circle.

Aunt Martha Bakely was friendly, plump, with a lined pink face that obviously had once been pretty. And she liked cooking for men. She had been distressed after her husband's death and hadn't cooked much until Janie came to live with her.

At the sight of John Slocum, her surprisingly clear blue eyes opened saucer-wide. "Well, you're a fine-sized man. Big, like my husband, Ethan. You probably have the appetite he had."

Slocum grinned. "Well, Aunt Martha, nobody's ever complained about my appetite."

51

"Aunt Martha is the best cook in Cragg City," said Jane.

Slocum looked at the pink-faced lady. "It's been a long time since I had a real home-cooked meal."

They had a dinner of Southern fried chicken, with chitlin's, black-eyed peas, collards, yams, biscuits, and pecan pie for dessert, all prepared with tender love, which Slocum enjoyed hugely. Janie then suggested that she and Slocum have more coffee outside the house, at a table facing the western stretch of the mountain.

Slocum sipped his coffee and looked into Jane's dark blue eyes, then at the blue cast of the darkening sky; they seemed to match.

"I suppose," she said, "you've been over to Braddock."

He nodded.

She gazed at him. "He pays big money for what he wants. Did you sign up?"

"Not yet."

She toyed with her coffee cup. "Why not? Most gunmen would snap at the offer." And she studied him closely.

Slocum looked out at the darkening sky, glints of gold striking the mountain peaks.

"I don't like the men around Braddock. Like Sykes."

"You know him?"

"I knew him in Waco. A bounty hunter. A killer."

"There's plenty like him around Braddock." Her voice was cold. She glanced at the bandage on his arm. "I've been meaning to ask. What's that?"

"One of Braddock's boys shot at me. You know the gent. We met him at the cafe. Willie. He was with Frank, the one who knocked you down."

"Willie shot at you?"

"Just a scratch."

She gazed at him. "What happened after that?"

Slocum raised his coffee cup and spoke in a dry voice. "I let him think he got me and tracked him down. He looked surprised, expecting me to be dead. 'It'd be nice to kill you twice,' he said." Slocum paused.

"Then what?"

"I gave him a nice burial."

Her eyes stayed on him. "Life is somewhat uncertain out here." She looked at his empty coffee cup. "Perhaps you'd like something stronger."

"I might."

She went into the house and he looked around at her land, some cows and chickens and the corral with a couple of horses. The land wasn't big, but the grass looked well-nourished from the meandering stream.

She came out with a bottle of whiskey, and he liked the casual grace of her walk. She wore a fringed buckskin jacket and Levi's that neatly fitted her fine figure. She put the bottle on the table.

He poured some whiskey into his coffee. "Gives it a kick." He sipped it. "You don't like Braddock?"

Her blue eyes glittered, and she looked at the distant peaks. "He's mean-hearted. He's got a big spread, but craves this one. My aunt has lived here since long before Braddock came out. And he's tried to get it every which way. Made fancy offers,

and he blusters. If we were men, he'd have us shot.
We're not selling."

"Why?" Slocum gave her a stare. "You probably
could use the money to get better land. You'd get
him off your back. A man like him is dangerous."

She looked sharply at him. "Yes, he can be dangerous."

"So take his money and find something else."

"I told you, we don't need money. Martha is at-
tached to this land. Her husband is buried here. She
has memories. And what would she do with the
money? She wants to be left in peace."

Slocum grimaced. "You can't get much peace if
you got what a man like Braddock wants."

Her hand brushed lightly at her rich auburn hair
as she looked at him with narrowed eyes. "You
seem to know Braddock pretty good. And you're
arguing for him."

"I've met men like Braddock. And I wouldn't
like to see you or your aunt get hurt."

She studied him. "That sounds kind. But I
wonder. Perhaps Honey is the reason. They say she
has persuading ways."

He grinned. "I'm sure she does."

Jane's eyes glittered suddenly. "Got a way of falling easy on her back, I hear."

Slocum was startled. "That's not a nice thing for
a well-bred Texas girl to say."

"I'm not well-bred. And not a Texas girl."

He laughed. "Don't know what you are, but
you've got plenty of spunk."

Her eyes gleamed as if with sudden pleasure.
"Does that mean you won't join Braddock?"

"I might stay on the sidelines. To see what happens."

She leaned back, her face solemn. "At least you're not with him. I'd hate to fight you, too."

He stared. "How can someone like you, almost alone, stand up against his power?"

She looked away, then at him, an intense look. "I suppose I could use all the help I can get."

"But who's goin' to buck Braddock?"

After a silence, she said slowly, "Only the brave. Only the brave."

Midway in the sky the moon glowed like a big silver globe as Slocum rode toward town. He felt good. It was not often that he enjoyed the privilege of eating a fine home-cooked dinner. His diet on the trail was mostly jerky, beans, or whatever he could shoot on the hoof. Tonight he had dined well, and he felt grateful.

He glanced about at the lonely land. The brush, the cactus, and the crags in the glitter of the moonlight made a ghostly landscape.

Slocum's thoughts began to circle around Jane Bakely. She intrigued him. She was one cool and collected lady. Not someone easily rattled. She didn't shake much before Braddock's muscle. It was easy to see she was ready to stand up to him, a ruthless man who'd ride roughshod over anyone to get what he wanted. Even over women. Slocum was convinced that if a man owned the Bakely land, he would have departed fast and long ago or he'd be pushing daisies. But two women presented Braddock with a delicate problem. Even in this wild ter-

ritory, you didn't stampede over women. Slocum
felt that if Braddock couldn't persuade the Bakelys
to sell, some unfortunate accident would befall the
ladies. Slocum felt he knew the Braddocks of this
world.

There didn't seem much that Braddock feared.
He had lined up some fast gunslingers, so why
should he fear? But Slocum remembered that Braddock seemed a bit edgy about the masked kid. Was
that a chink in Braddock's armor?

What had he said? "*Rustlers were just stealin', but
the kid was killin'.*" True enough. But why should
that spook him? The kid had killed decent citizens,
Braddock said. It was puzzling. A fast mystery gunman riding after stages, forcing a picked man to pull
his gun. Not exactly a nice thing to do, even if in the
code of the territory it wasn't called murder. It'd be
nice to find out what was eating the kid.

He'd turn up again—Slocum was sure of it. But
if the kid had to face a posse with Sykes, Frank, and
the other fast guns, he'd come tumbling down. Slocum shook his head. It was a pity. He had a curious
liking for the kid—he had style, and an elegant
way. He just didn't seem to be a low-down murder-
ing dog.

By now Slocum had reached the edge of town; it
was lit up and sounded merry. Cowboys loitered in
the streets, and the sound of laughter floated from
Hardy's Saloon. Slocum rode to the rail, dismounted, and walked through the saloon doors,
where the smell of whiskey, sweat, and tobacco
smoke hit him. Cowboys from surrounding ranches
came for the pleasures of drink, gambling, and

women. They worked hard on the range during the day, and now they wanted play.

Slocum moved through the bunch of men at the bar and found a space. Hardy, a bald, cheerful man with gartered sleeves, came over and planted a whiskey bottle and a glass in front of him.

Slocum drank two shots, which seemed to clear the dust from his throat. Elbows on the bar edge, he turned to look around. Men were gambling at the tables, and women in garish dresses lolled about. Braddock's men were playing cards—a husky, hard-looking lot. Among them were Sykes and Frank, the sidekick of Willie, who was now pushing up daisies. Frank, with his back to the bar, had not seen him yet. Then Sykes smiled, beckoning him. Slocum drifted over with his drink.

"Hello, Slocum. Feel like losin' money?"

"I feel like playin', but not losin." He glanced at Frank, who was staring at him. Frank had been surprised at Sykes's greeting. Sykes was his boss, but Slocum was a man very much on Frank's mind.

"Been lookin' for you, mister," Frank growled. He pushed back his chair, standing with hands at his side.

Sykes, instantly grasping the situation, stared at Frank. "Sit down, Frank," he said coldly.

Frank's jaw hardened. "I've got a score to settle with this cowboy, Sykes."

"Sit down, Frank." Sykes's voice was frigid, his mouth taut.

Frank took a deep breath, glanced at Slocum, then sat down.

Sykes stroked his chin. "Mr. Braddock wants

Slocum to come in with us. And what Braddock wants, I want. So whatever is eatin' you, Frank, just sit on it." He turned to Slocum. "I was sayin', maybe you'd like to play."

Slocum nodded. "Don't mind if I do."

Frank growled in his throat.

Sykes looked at him.

"Okay," Frank said. "At least there's nothin' wrong with his money."

Slocum smiled. "Yeah, why don't you try and get some of it, mister?"

They made space for him, and Sykes began to deal. As they played, Sykes introduced the players —Slats, Chet, Moose, Lefty, and Ray, all gunmen who worked for Braddock. To Slocum's practiced eye, they wére a brutal bunch of hardcases, men with the bruises and scars of countless fights and gun battles in some of the toughest towns in the territory.

After a few deals, Sykes spoke softly to Slocum. "Made up your mind yet?"

Slocum smiled. "Not yet. Still thinkin'.'"

Sykes grinned. "It's a good deal, Slocum. Better than bounty huntin'. You don't bust your ass trackin' in the blistering sun day after day. You get good money. Good eats. Good backup. These are all picked men, fast guns. Can't see much reason to hesitate."

Slocum just shrugged good-naturedly and looked at his cards.

"Reckon I can see his reason," said Frank.

Sykes turned slowly to look at him, as did the others at the table.

Frank's teeth glittered under his mustache. "The cowboy is sweet on the Bakely girl."

Sykes scowled; he didn't like that. He knew that Braddock wanted the Bakely land. And he figured that Slocum could be touchy about the girl, especially talked about in a place like this.

Slocum had cast an icy eye on Frank, so Sykes spoke quickly. "Don't mind that polecat, Slocum. It's mighty easy to be sweet on the Bakely girl. Now, let's play poker."

Slocum picked up his drink. Frank was a nasty hombre whose pride had been badly damaged. He didn't forgive a knockdown. Sooner or later he'd demand a showdown. And in a way, it might be better to have one straight on. Frank might believe, like his sidekick Willie, that there was a better payoff in back-shooting.

Frank looked at Sykes, then drawled. "We gotta remember that Mr. Braddock doesn't care much for the Bakely folk."

"It's the land he cares about, Frank. He's got nothin' against the Bakelys. They'll sell in time."

"Maybe not."

"Let's play poker," growled Moose, a big man with a broad, heavy-jawed face.

"Yeah," said the others. "Let's play."

It wasn't long after this that Slocum's luck turned, and he began to win. In one pot, he got a pair of fives, then, to his pleasure, pulled another two on his draw.

He upped the betting, and everyone dropped but Frank, who liked his cards. Slocum remembered he had stood pat. He stared into Frank's eyes, into

their depths, and what he saw made him kick up the betting. Frank might have good cards, but he wanted more the joy of rubbing Slocum's nose in the dust. And maybe he believed Slocum was bluffing.

A hundred and thirty dollars piled up on the table before they were ready to show cards.

Frank showed a full house—three queens, two tens—and he grinned triumphantly. He stared into Slocum's face and reached out for the pot.

Then Slocum showed four fives.

"Poker is a game of skill, Frank," Slocum said in a silky voice, and he started to rake in the money.

Frank stared at the cards disbelievingly. He was in shock. He'd been convinced that Slocum had been bluffing. He watched Slocum move the money out of his reach and a flush of red appeared in his cheeks. "Damn you," he muttered. "You're my hoodoo." And he went for his gun.

Slocum, who understood the rage of defeat and what it could do to a man, was ready. Nothing he did was waste motion. His hand moved, a streak of lightning, and his gun was firing in a split second.

Frank, a fast gun, got his finger on the trigger, but the barrel never came up. He staggered under Slocum's bullet. Shock hit his eyes as he put his hand to his chest and pulled it away, bloody. He staggered again, falling over his chair, going down to the floor slowly. There he squirmed and realized he was dying. His black fading eyes fastened on one man.

"Kill him for me, Moose," he whispered.

Then Frank died.

Slocum, still holding his gun, threw a glance at Moose, who looked stunned at the sudden death. Frank, in his last moment, had passed the torch to Moose, a brutal cowboy. What would he do? Grab his gun or bide his time or forget the whole thing? It had been Frank who went for his gun first. He might have ties with these men. Moose looked jolted, as did they all, Slocum thought. No matter how tough you were, the sight of death, especially of a man you knew, who minutes ago was talking and drinking and now was lying like dead meat on the saloon floor—that had to jar you. For a split second Slocum's own life had been threatened. A split second slower and *he* might have been the dead meat.

The barkeeper, Hardy, quickly ordered two men to clear away the body, an event that happened more than once on nights crowded with drinking, wild cowboys packing hardware.

"Sit down, sit down, Slocum," Sykes said. "We still got a game goin'."

Slocum holstered his gun and sat down, his eyes traveling slowly around the table. These were hard-faced gunmen, and Frank had been one of them. Moose, Lefty, and Chet were staring at him, and Slocum sensed hostility. You settle with one, he thought, and three spring up. Sykes, however, looked easy. In fact, he seemed secretly pleased. Why? Maybe Frank had been a hard nut and Sykes was glad to be rid of him.

Sykes, too, looked at his men. "Frank was a bad loser. If you pull your gun every time you lose, there won't be many poker players around." He

shuffled the cards, then turned to Slocum. "Frank was one of our fast guns, Slocum. Braddock won't like it much that we lost him." He toyed with the cards. "Of course, if I could tell him we picked up a faster gun than Frank, that'd make him happy."

Slocum picked up his shot glass and emptied it. "I'll make up my mind in a day or so." The death of this polecat had nothing to do with his decision. He stood. "Excuse me, gents. I reckon I've had enough poker for the night."

As he walked away from the table, he felt their eyes boring into his back. Moose, Lefty, and Chet —he'd have to keep an eye on these critters.

As he passed the bar, some men smiled. There were always cowboys who got a kick out of a shooting match, Slocum thought. It was the ultimate entertainment—life and death.

He walked out of the smoky saloon into the clear summer night with its sweet smell of grass. Thousands of big silver stars sparkled on the deep blue coat of the sky.

Slocum took a deep breath and started for the hotel and a good night's sleep.

5

Next morning, Slocum rode out of town heading south. In the distance he could see the vast walls of stone, with their sharp needle peaks that, hit by the light of the sun, looked like dazzling lances aimed at the sky.

As he rode, he thought about Braddock, who wanted him to join up fast. Slocum felt it hadn't been smart to commit himself to a quick decision. He wasn't that clear in his mind. His sympathies lay with Jane Bakely.

There was something fine the way she stood alone against Braddock's power and money. But it was foolish for the Bakelys to stay put. Sooner or later Braddock would run over them. The odds against Jane were overwhelming.

Only the brave, she had said, would stand alongside her. The brave and the foolish. Still, it was a

pity that Aunt Martha was being pushed to abandon the land where her husband lay buried, where she had happy memories. What could he do for them? Braddock was a hard hombre; he needed the water, and wasn't going to give it up because an old lady had sentimental memories about her dead husband.

Slocum shook his head.

He reached the edge of high ground, swung off his horse, and pulled his canteen to quench his thirst. It was a beautiful spot with a long view of the valley below. Sticking to his train of thought, he wondered if he just might help Jane by joining Braddock. If he knew the man's plans, he might do something to protect the girl and her aunt.

Then he heard the voices floating up from directly below him, where the trail passed against the side of the cliff. One voice sounded familiar. He crept silently to the edge and looked down, and his eyes widened.

Not that far below was the Masked Kid confronted by what looked like two rustlers. From what he could judge, they had just come abreast each other on the trail. Nobody had a gun out.

The Kid was still in his saddle, looking at them, but he didn't seem uneasy.

"Well," said the rustler with a scraggly beard, "you look like a young fella with money. You might want to help a coupla cowboys down on their luck."

"How can I help you?" the Kid asked politely.

"That's a nice way to talk. Don't you think so, Lem?"

"Yeah, Jess, he talks real nice," said Lem, a nar-

row-faced man with a stubble beard and a rumpled black hat.

"So why don't you toss me your money?" Jess said. Then he stroked his face and, with a wicked grin, added, "You might ask, Why the hell should I do that?" He turned mockingly to his sidekick. "Why should he do that, Lem?"

Lem grinned, amused by the fun of it. "'Cause we got two guns and he's got one, and we'd blast the hell outa him."

The grin on Jess's shaggy face broadened. "That's why, young fella."

The Masked Kid looked at them, thinking hard, then he slowly reached into his pocket and tossed his wallet at Lem, who caught it deftly. Jess kept his eye on the Kid.

Slocum, who had a ringside seat on the high crag, could hear them clearly as their voices spiraled up. He had to smile: this was a switch. The kid usually did the holdup, but he didn't steal.

Now what would happen? Slocum wondered. He studied the two polecats, who looked amused at the slender Kid who wore a mask. He had thrown his money, as if he didn't care to have an encounter, just wanted to get past them.

The drifters looked easy. They had the Kid outnumbered, and he looked almost juvenile.

Then Jess, the one with a straggly beard, spoke in a husky voice. "Now that we got your dough, Kid, why don't you give us a look at your mug. Let's see what you look like."

There was a long pause. "You've got my money,

mister. That oughta satisfy you. Why don't you let me go on about my business."

"What is your business? Robbin'?"

The Kid seemed to stare. "No, it's not me that's robbing." His voice was calm. "But my business is not your business. So why don't you let me ride on."

The scraggy beard kept his eyes on the Kid, but spoke to his partner. "What do you think, Lem? We got his money. Should we let him stay behind that mask? Don't seem right."

"It ain't right, Jess. What's he got to hide? I'd like a look at him. No, young fella, jest slip that mask down. We're showing our faces. Show yours."

Again that silence. The Kid seemed to be staring through his mask at them. "I'm goin' to ride."

"I wouldn't advise that," said Jess.

"Why should you want to stop me?"

"I'm a mighty curious man," said Jess, and he leered.

"You could be mighty dead," said the Kid.

There was a long silence, then both men burst out laughing. Jess even looked at Lem, roaring, then suddenly went for his gun. The Kid's move was streaked lightning. The bullet hit Jess in the pistol hand, cracking his bone. He yelled and dropped his gun.

Lem just watched, petrified.

The Kid swung his gun on him. "Throw your gun, Lem. Far off."

Lem pulled his gun and flung it, watching the Kid, his eyes wide with fear. He'd been stunned by the Kid's fast draw.

"Now toss me my wallet. You didn't know when you were ahead," the Kid said calmly.

White-faced, Lem brought out the wallet.

"Get riding," the Kid ordered.

Jess, holding his hand, grimaced with pain as he kicked the haunches of his horse, throwing a fearful glance over his shoulder. The Kid watched them ride north. After they had disappeared round a bend, the Kid glanced up at the sun, then started to ride south.

Slocum shook his head. He'd been ready to interfere, but there was something about that Kid. Well, he sure could take care of himself.

In fact, he was one hot pistol.

Slocum idly trailed the Kid, staying out of sight. Where was the kid headed? What was he after? He was a streak with his gun, but he seemed to use it only when he had to.

Those two polecats, for example, who wanted his money. The Kid gave it rather than fight. The money didn't seem important; but when they wanted a look under the mask, he pulled his gun and struck quick as a rattler.

He sure wanted to stay behind that mask.

Slocum smiled. He had seen the Kid stop two stagecoaches and shoot two men dead. Yet it was hard to think of him as a killer. He could have shot Jess dead, but didn't. Seemed like only when he trapped a special man did he become a cold-blooded killer. It was mystifying.

It was hot. There were hot crags to his left, thick brush and small trees around him. The earth seemed to swelter. Slocum glanced at the trail, then

decided to stop tracking. He'd go back to town. But first he'd eat. He had shot a jackrabbit, and now he fried it. After eating, Slocum leaned against a rock and looked at the land shimmering in heat. His eyes wearied, and he dozed.

Then he heard the soft step. His hand went instinctively to his gun as his eyes snapped open. But it was too late. The man had a gun on him.

"Pull your gun gently, and throw it here." The man had a heavy mustache that drooped, pale eyes in a flushed drinker's face. A beat-up bowler nestled on his head.

Slocum threw his gun. A thievin' hyena, he guessed.

The man looked grim. "Doesn't pay to sleep in these parts, mister."

"What do you want?"

The hyena grinned devilishly. "I'll tell you what. Your horse is a beauty. That's what I want."

"No. You don't want him." Slocum's voice was cold.

The pale washed-out eyes stared. "Yeah, I want him. I know someone who'd pay fancy money for him."

Slocum leaned forward. Was he in the rustler gang that preyed on Braddock's horses? The rustler's own horse was tethered in the brush. "I don't think you oughta take him."

"Oh, you don't. You're lucky I don't shoot you."

"You goin' to leave me without a horse in this heat?"

"Yeah, ain't it a pity? You don't think I'm gonna give you my horse. I ain't stupid. You'd come after

me." He grinned savagely, stroking his mustache. "I told you it's not smart to sleep in these parts."

Then he moved to the roan and swung over the saddle.

Slocum watched in fury, helpless without his gun.

The rustler stared hard at Slocum. "You look ornery. Maybe it's better, after all, to put you outa business." He raised his gun to shoot.

A shot cracked from the high crags nearby.

The rustler jumped crazily in the saddle, then went down, twisting on the ground.

Slocum threw a quick look up at the crag.

It was the Masked Kid, sitting calmly on his horse, holding a rifle.

The rustler lay sprawled on the ground, his chest red with blood. He was lucky, Slocum thought. Horse thieves were lynched.

Slocum looked up.

The Kid looked for a long moment, waved his hand, a friendly gesture, turned his horse, and passed down behind rocks, out of sight.

As Slocum rode back toward town he felt gratitude to the kid. The kid had saved his life, and his beloved roan. Though Slocum would have labored with might and main to track the horse, rustlers had a way of making them disappear. Yes, he was beholden to the kid. But his curiosity was strongly stirred. Who the hell was he, and why did he hide behind a mask? Someday that riddle would be solved.

As he rode into town, it was mid-afternoon—closing time for the bank. Customers were coming

out, as did Braddock and Sykes. It was Braddock's bank, and the kind of man he was, Slocum figured, Braddock was in there often, counting the money.

Braddock spoke in a low voice to Sykes, then waved at Slocum. He came down off the horse.

"Well, mister," said Braddock, with an almost venomous stare, "what's it gonna be? You with us?"

He's asking, Are you with us or against us? Slocum thought. Braddock, in spite of his phony friendliness, was a bull underneath. Why else would he collect top gunmen like Sykes, Moose, and Lefty if not to mow down those who stood against him?

"Yeah," Sykes said. "You'd best come in with us, Slocum. I told Mr. Braddock here you're the smartest gun I seen around. Other than me, o'course," he added with an ironic smile. "But we won't argue that."

Sykes stroked his chin. "Anyway, the best rustler I ever saw is Charley Devlin, and he has a mean bunch. They been tearing a chunk out of Mr. Braddock's herds. We gotta box 'em in and wipe 'em out. We been collecting good men. If you come in, Slocum, you'll work as top man under me." He turned to Braddock. "Won't nobody be able to stand against us if you get this man."

Braddock was impressed. He'd been studying Slocum, looking at the sinewy lean lines, the cut of his jaw, the steady glitter of the green eyes. A good man to have on your side, he thought.

"Listen, cowboy. I ain't a cheapskate when it come to hiring an ace gun. I was offering you two hundred a month. Okay, I'll kick it up to two-fifty. Now that's unbeatable pay, so let's clinch the deal."

Then Slocum made up his mind. He had been thinking, the closer you got to your enemy, the better you could protect your friends. When Braddock would move against Jane Bakely, he'd get the tipoff and be able to help her. You didn't owe loyalty to men such as Braddock.

"Okay," he said.

Braddock grinned ear to ear. "You won't be sorry, Slocum." His eyes gleamed with satisfaction. "Okay, Sykes, it's your show. Go after Devlin and his mangy bunch. Tear 'em apart. We've got to send out a message to these rotten, thievin' dogs: 'If you steal a Braddock brand, you stretch your neck.'" He glanced at both Sykes and Slocum. "Don't have to tell you boys. Main thing is, don't shoot 'em. String 'em up and let them hang. A taste of hangin' is the best cure for rustlers."

He reached into his shirt pocket, pulled out a cigar, and lit it. Then his face took on a malevolent gleam. "And keep your eyes peeled for the Masked Kid. That killer is runnin' wild. Draggin' out decent men and shootin' 'em. He deserves no mercy. I want him hung on the highest tree. Hang him with his mask round his neck." He grinned viciously. "That will be a pretty sight. There's an extra hundred for the gun that gets him. Spread the word."

He started toward his horse, then turned suddenly. "Say, Honey will be tickled to hear you joined us, Slocum."

Sykes turned sharply to look at Slocum, a hostile gleam in his eyes. Then, as if aware he might have revealed his feelings, Sykes casually pulled the red

kerchief from around his neck and mopped his face. "We'll meet out at the ranch after sunup tomorrow and go on a hunt for the Devlin bunch. I have a notion where to look."

Though Sykes seemed as friendly as before, a new edge had crept into his voice, Slocum thought.

That night, in his hotel room, Slocum was in a somber mood. He looked out the window. The moon was a thin sliver, and the sky was clustered with big stars far as his eye could see.

In the distance, in the soft moonlight, the mountain, with the print of eternity on its massive stone, loomed up mysteriously.

The street was deserted except for two cowboys staggering toward a loaded buckboard. Their voices were low, as if they felt it indecent to be drunk on Main Street this late. Slocum watched them climb precariously to the seat. The driver snapped his whip, the horses strained, and the springs groaned as the buckboard rumbled on the rutted ground.

Though Slocum's green eyes followed them, he was thinking of Braddock. The man had a right to protect his property, and a cowboy who rustled knew he was gambling with lynching.

But Slocum had to wonder at Braddock's ferocity toward the Masked Kid. Wanting him lynched on sight, ready to pay a fancy fee to the killer. Why did Braddock want the Kid dead? Because he was knocking off decent citizens, he said. But how decent was Braddock, who was ready to run two women off their legal land to grab their water? A bit strange, wasn't it?

And what about Sykes—the way he had come up sharp when Braddock mentioned that Honey would be pleased? Was Sykes sweet on Honey? If so, he wouldn't care for competition. A woman like Honey could start up a hornets' nest. Sykes had been friendly up to now, but Slocum sensed this could change.

Slocum sighed and turned to the bed.

After a day like this, the bed looked good.

Sunlit clouds stretched massively across the sky as Slocum rode the roan toward the Braddock ranch. He was on his way to join Sykes and his boys. Object: to knock out Charley Devlin and his gang of rustlers. Not that Slocum cared about saving the Braddock stock. But rustlers were a bad breed and you couldn't let them run wild or nobody's stock would be safe. In the West, rustling was the meanest, most ornery thing a man could do. You didn't shoot rustlers, you hung them.

Slocum thought of Charley Devlin, whom he had met once in a card game at the Alhambra in Tombstone. A burly man with stony eyes that didn't reveal the thoughts behind them. He played smart cards, bluffed cleverly, won a packet that day. He'd come out of Kansas, out of the troubles, a tough, gun-fast cowboy who decided money was on the wrong side of the law. He recruited a rough gang and for a time did gun-running at the border, selling to the revolutionaries. He got chased back to Texas, then turned to rustling.

That was Devlin, and they were going after him in the badlands. Not easy, smoking him out.

Slocum pulled on the reins of the roan and mopped his sweating brow with his kerchief. The Braddock ranch lay a couple of miles south. He was on a high slope and could see the mountain in the distance, the rises and small valleys, ridges and hollows. Around him were juniper, blue spruce, and cottonwoods.

Then he saw the gray mare come out from behind a boulder, and riding it was a girl with auburn hair that burned in the sun. She had spotted him, and she waved.

As he rode toward her, he couldn't help puzzle how she happened to be here, and if it was a chance meeting.

"Well," he said, "where's the pretty filly going?"

Honey swung off her horse and stood facing him, with a smile of a cat about to swallow the mouse. "Sometimes you don't know where you're going until you get there."

He got off the roan and walked toward her. "Didn't expect to find you out here."

"That's funny. 'Cause I expected to find you out here." She had that same smile.

Then it wasn't chance. He looked at her full lips, her curving body with its full breasts—every inch a honey. He felt tingles in his groin.

She was watching him. "I heard Sykes mention that you had joined the Braddock bunch and you were riding out, so I thought I'd come out to show you my pleasure."

She moved close, her blue eyes gleaming with anticipated excitement. One sexy lady, Slocum thought. His body felt primed. She brought her face

up to his, put out her full lips for kissing, her breasts pressing against him, firm and full. He slipped his hand into her shirt, feeling the silk of her skin, the taut nipple. He opened her shirt, looked at the two beauties, leaned down to put his tongue to the nipple. She heaved a sigh, and her hands went down to his britches. She stroked him, and it wasn't long before they pitched their clothes. She had a great body—long slender legs, rounded hips, full breasts. His hands moved over her breasts, down to her fine buttocks. He explored her, and she groaned with passion. He kept stroking until she went for him with a hunger almost wolfish.

She kept at it, then he brought her gently to the earth. She shuddered when he went into her. He began to move, and her eyes glazed, like a woman in a dream. He kept at it, his pleasure sharpening, and she tightened as if with pain. Finally he made his big move, felt the pulsations, and she let out a small screech and her nails dug into him.

After she had dressed and simmered down, she looked at him with a curious smile. "I figure, Slocum, I owed you a reward for joining up."

He couldn't help but grin. The way she carried on, the reward seemed to go two ways. She sure liked her sex.

They walked to their horses, and he thought of Sykes, who had a yen for her. "You say Sykes is waiting?"

She nodded. "Getting the boys together to go after Devlin. Goin' to nail that buzzard to the nearest tree."

"What do you think of Sykes?" he asked casually.

She looked startled, then, as a memory trailed through her mind, she said, "He's a lot of man. Like you, Slocum. Must say I have a weakness for red-blooded men." She looked at him. "Why'd you ask?"

"Just curious." She had a weakness for men, all right. Trouble was, Slocum suspected, a man like Sykes also had a weakness—jealousy. And Honey was a filly who didn't particularly mind sparking jealous excitement among her men—it enlivened her life. He'd have to be careful about Sykes.

They rode back to the ranch together, and he saw Sykes and four men sitting on the fence of the corral, watching a rider breaking in a brown bronc.

Sykes glanced casually at them, and Slocum thought he caught a bit of frost in his eye. Was he smart enough to figure that hotpants Honey had ridden out to give Slocum a warm welcome?

She jerked her thumb at Slocum. "I was ridin' west and stumbled into this one," she said easily, not caring what Sykes thought. Or maybe she liked to put the edge between men.

But Sykes didn't tip his hand. "We been waitin' for him," he said. A sharp poker player, Slocum thought, who kept his cards close to his chest. A man who kept a lid on his feelings was the most dangerous of all.

Honey smiled brightly, her blue eyes staying on Sykes, curious to see the impact. She waved at the men and walked toward the big white ranch house, her riding pants tight about her full buttocks. The men watched her.

Slocum moved toward Skyes and got a foot up on the corral fence next to him.

Skyes lit a cigarillo. "Won't be long before we start. We're waiting for a couple of men to come in off the range, Moose and Lefty, two good hands to have on this job."

Slocum nodded, remembering that before he croaked, Frank had tossed the torch to Moose, a brutal-looking cowboy. As Slocum watched the rider working the bronc in the corral, he wondered if a man like Moose would pull his gun and honor his sidekick's dying wish. In Slocum's experience, men like Moose acted only if there was money in it. Not a man to risk his neck for nothing. But you couldn't be certain. Moose, on impulse, if he found Slocum's back an easy target, might just throw a bullet for his old sidekick, Frank.

Slocum decided it would be smart to watch this polecat, too. In his decision to be helpful to Janie, he had joined a bunch of killers who'd just as soon make him their target.

Sykes scanned the horizon for Moose and Lefty. He turned to Slocum. "You know Charley Devlin, I reckon."

Slocum nodded. "Met him once in Tombstone."

Sykes's eyes glinted. "A wily dog. We've been hunting him. Somehow he gets wind of our moves and he's gone." He spotted two riders coming from the east, moved off the fence, and stretched. "We've got a line on his hideout, a tip. We nailed one of his men and squeezed it outa his hide." Sykes's thin lips wreathed in a grin at the memory. "Devlin's up in the hills, and if we move fast, we'll

snare him and stretch his neck on the nearest tree."

Moose and Lefty rode up in a bit of dust and came off their horses. At the sight of Slocum, Moose's brutal features twisted in a scowl. Slocum gazed at him calmly. Moose was not a man to camouflage his feelings, like Sykes. You knew exactly where you stood with him.

Moose jerked a finger at Slocum. "Is he ridin' with us?"

"That's what he's here for, Moose," Sykes said. "Any objections?"

Moose's small brown eyes smoldered. "It's just that he shot Frankie. And now he's ridin' with us. Don't add up."

"It adds up this way, Moose. Braddock wants him. And what Braddock wants, he gets. That's what I'm here for."

Moose threw a mean glance at Slocum. "Don't expect me to be happy about it."

"Just do your job, Moose. That's what you're being paid for," Sykes said.

They rode for miles into hilly country under a sun that became fierce in the afternoon. It drilled down on the land, and the coyotes slunk into whatever shade they could find.

Moose cursed at the heat and complained it was a rotten day to hunt for rustlers.

Sykes mopped the sweat off his broad face with his soiled red neckerchief. "Any day is a good day to catch a rustler. Right, Slocum?"

Slocum nodded, thinking that as far as he was concerned, rustling stock from Braddock wasn't all

that bad. The roan's ears went up. "Water nearby."

When they reached a small stream, they drank, filled their canteens, and Slocum washed up. Then they sat in the shade of a cottonwood and ate jerky and drank whiskey.

Sykes looked at his men—five, counting himself and Slocum. The good guns were Lefty, Moose, and Sam, who was part Comanche, it was said; he could track a coyote to hell and back.

"We're headed for Devlin's hideaway cabin. It's off Parsons Creek." Sykes told them, then grinned sadistically. "I got it from Hildy Jones, after we worked him over. He sure made a mistake, comin' into Cragg City. I knew Hildy was tied up with Devlin. They were sidekicks years ago, back in Tombstone. The layout is that the cabin's on a hill. There's an approach, with a lookout. It's your job, Sam, to sneak up on him, like you do so good. Then . . ." He made a slicing motion with his finger across his neck.

"The idea is to get Devlin alive and bring him back near town and string him up so folks can see. Teach it don't pay to steal from the Braddocks."

He rubbed his chin thoughtfully. "Devlin don't work with more than four men; he don't like to share profits. And Hildy's out. So the opposition ain't tough. But Devlin's smart and slippery. There's been a lasso out for him for a long time, but nobody's grabbed him. It's only 'cause I recognized Hildy that we were able to pinpoint Devlin's hideaway."

Sykes glanced at Slocum, a look that Slocum thought almost evil. Then he said, "What happens

after we get the lookout? Slocum, you and Sam will put up a strong front. Me and the boys will circle round and nail Devlin if he tries to run the back trail." His smoky brown eyes stayed fixed on Slocum, then he turned away.

Slocum smoothed his hand over the grass. A piece of cheap trickery, he thought. Just as he suspected, Sykes was a jealous dog, but a good player when it came to hiding his hand. Didn't take much for Sykes to realize that Slocum, riding in with Honey, had been riding in her saddle. And he didn't like that. But he hadn't tipped his hand until now. You don't have to shoot your enemy, just put him in the front lines.

Devlin, as Slocum well knew, was not only smart but a deadeye. His hideaway was on high ground, with a command view.

Slocum stared into Sykes's eyes and could see the cunning deep down. "Why risk a front attack?" Slocum asked. "Why not come in quiet on the circle?"

Sykes, with a devilish grin, scratched his lean cheek. "I reckon you're askin' why put a strong gun like you, Slocum, up front. That's the idea. You put up some sharp fire and he runs. Makes it easier to grab him from behind, with his whole skin. We know it's harder to bring a polecat in alive than dead. Okay, let's ride."

Up on the slope in his hideaway cabin, Charley Devlin was playing cards with his burly sidekicks, Max and Lonnie. As usual, Devlin was winning because he played smart poker, but it didn't make him happy. He was broad-faced, broad-shouldered, with

stony dark eyes, and right now they brooded. Something was on his mind.

He suddenly tired of the game, cursed, and pushed his chair back. Max and Lonnie glanced at each other, then watched him silently. Devlin picked up the whiskey bottle and took a long swig. It burned his throat, but he liked the taste. He had a taste for whiskey, women, and the things money could buy. He walked to the door and looked down the slope, with its shrubs and small boulders. It looked clear enough under a smoky hot sun.

He gazed far out at the land, the great land, and he thought about himself. He hadn't been like other men, settlers who got some acres, some stock, and through sweat built it up. Work like a horse, then one day you'd find yourself with a bullet in your gut. So what'd you get for your pains? No, Devlin figured, let the other slob work and collect stock. Then he, Devlin, would come along and take off a piece. In all things you played the percentages, like you did in poker. Take Braddock. That big-shot polecat had more stock than any man deserved; he ought to want to share his wealth with his less fortunate brothers.

Devlin grinned. That's why he had borrowed Braddock's horses and sold them, sometimes across the border. Wasn't like stealin' from some broken-down cowboy with a small stake. No, Devlin felt all right about rustling Braddock.

Devlin's eyes narrowed. Of course, men like Braddock were greedy: the more they had, the more they wanted. They hated to share, which made Braddock dangerous. Devlin always knew

that a rustler's occupational risk was a noose, which made him mighty careful. He'd kept his neck unstretched because he kept his head clear, and in Kansas he'd slipped out of so many tight spots they called him slippery Devlin. He'd just delivered stock, been paid, and come back to his hideaway.

Then, looking out the window, he saw Lem and Jess ride up. He watched them dismount and walk toward the cabin, a couple of run-down polecats he'd picked up in Kansas. Jess pushed open the door and made a beeline for the whiskey. He raised the bottle to his lips and swallowed three big gulps.

Devlin stared at his shooting hand, bloody and bandaged with his neckerchief. "What the hell hit you?"

Jess looked surly. He just sat at the table with the bottle.

Devlin turned to Lem.

"He tangled with a hotshot kid, that's what hit him," Lem said.

"What do you mean?"

Lem thought carefully. He didn't want to tell Devlin they were picking the Kid's pocket. "We ran across a kid who looked like an easy mark. He had a fine horse. But Jess here got curious because the Kid was wearing a mask. Jess told him to take it off. He wanted a look at his mug. The Kid didn't like it and went for his gun."

Devlin thought about it. "The Masked Kid. I been hearing about him. Holdin' up stages and shootin' hell out of some polecat ridin' inside. No robbin'."

"That's him," Lem said. "And he shoots fast."

Devlin thought about him. "Wonder what his game is?"

Then he stared hard at Jess and his bloody hand. "You ain't any good to us now, mister. Not for a time."

Suddenly he wrenched his mind back to where it belonged, to what was bothering him during the poker game. And that was Hildy Jones, one of his key men. Where the hell was he? He'd gone to the way station to pick up supplies. He was overdue to be back, and there was no sign of him. A missing man set off Devlin's alarm instincts. Hildy was smart, but he had a fatal interest in the ladies, and in spite of his sworn intention not to go into Cragg City, he might have gone, just to sneak in a fast turn with Maisie, the saloon girl he liked. If he'd gone there, Devlin figured, anything could happen.

That's what preyed on his mind.

He turned to Lonnie. "Where the hell's Hildy?"

Lonnie, a husky cowboy with long black hair, scratched his stubble beard. "Probably guzzled too much and is sleepin' it off in some mangy hole."

Devlin looked at Max, a short, heavyset cowboy with a nose busted in a barroom brawl.

"That's what I think," Max said.

Devlin scowled. "He shoulda been back. What's holdin' him up? What if he got grabbed?" Devlin paused ominously.

Lonnie licked his lips.

Max scoffed. "Even so, he wouldn't talk. Not Hildy."

Devlin gritted his teeth. "Be surprised what a man'll do if he's pushed hard enough. This Brad-

dock's a mean dog. Been sayin' he's sick and tired of losin' horses."

Lonnie grinned. "Maybe sick and tired, but we just keep on rustlin' 'em."

Max looked at Devlin. "Maybe you're worrying too much, Dev."

"I worry just enough to keep our necks from gettin' stretched. Something's wrong. Hildy's supposed to be here and he's not. No matter what the reason, the main thing is he's not here. Lonnie, go out and see if everything's okay with Amos. You're almost due to take over his lookout anyway."

Lonnie shook his head. "I figure Hildy'll be ridin' in any minute. You're gettin' edgy for no reason, Dev."

Devlin glared. "Don't say that again."

Lonnie stood up and raised his hand placatingly. "Okay, okay." He picked up his hat, pushed open the door, and started down the slope, which curved at the bottom, where the lookout, Amos, was posted.

Amos was sitting on a stony ledge, smoking and thinking. It was late afternoon, and shadows were crawling trickily off the hillside, the rocks, and the shrubs. Amos felt bored, as he always did when he stood lookout. He didn't think lookout was needed, since the hideaway cabin was hidden fine.

They kept the rustled horses below in the corral, but it was empty now. Amos smiled. Braddock had fine horses, and they had fetched good prices. After the sale, the boys had gone to Caliente, where they had whored and guzzled for three whole days,

spending plenty. Then they'd come to this hideaway to recuperate from their riotous ventures.

The only cowpoke, Amos remembered, who hadn't laid up to rest was Hildy Jones. That polecat could screw till the cows came home. And Hildy, before he went for supplies to the way station, started to talk lustfully about Maisie, one of the party girls in Cragg. Amos shook his head. You'd think Hildy would've got his fill of women in Caliente. He was one helluva stud. Amos tired of the women and the drinkin' and was glad to get back to the peace of the hideaway. Except that lookout duty was dull as hell. Now he was watching the buzzards swoop down to feast on the kill of a cougar. Funny how those buzzards flew, their big wings riding the wind, and what an ugly mug they had, with a beak made for tearing.

Amos's thoughts wandered idly as the shadows lengthened. Then he noticed the rock. It was curious, but he hadn't seen that rock before. Was it because of the tricky shadows? he wondered. He felt irritated and glanced at the sun's position. Time for his relief, he thought. He was getting stare nutty. He turned back to the rock, but it wasn't a rock. It was Sam.

Amos grabbed for his rifle, but it was too late, for the silver flash hurtling through the air buried itself in his chest with a deadly *thump*. Amos, his body in a spasm, tried to pull out the knife, twisting and turning, then his eyes rolled in his head and he fell forward.

Sam walked casually toward the body. Then he

whistled a soft birdcall. From around the descending curve of land, Slocum appeared.

He glanced at the dead lookout, then began to climb. Sam had done his job. Now they'd go for the cabin, hidden up in the pines. By this time, Slocum thought, Sykes and his men must have reached the back trail, in case Devlin made a break for it.

Suddenly Slocum spotted a movement and hissed at Sam, who just had time to sprawl under some brush. Slocum slipped behind a boulder, from which he peered cautiously, watching the husky cowboy lumbering down through the brush. One of the rustlers, headed for the lookout? Why now? To relieve the lookout or for a double-check? If it was a check, then Devlin was feeling skittish about his missing man. In that case, he'd make fast moves.

Crouched behind his rock, Slocum was thinking that from now on you couldn't call the shots. Anything could happen.

When Lonnie didn't see Amos on lookout he sensed that something was wrong. He pulled his gun. "Amos?" he called.

No answer. Crouching, Lonnie came forward. Then, moving to a wider view, he saw the sprawled body. His face distorted, and, searching the ground nearby, he picked up Sam, trying to stay flat under a batch of brush. The rustler raised his gun to shoot.

That did it for Slocum. Devlin would be alerted by the shot anyway. Slocum's gun barked, and the rustler was thrown back. He lay still. Sam and Slocum moved quickly up the slope, to make headway before the men above would come down shooting.

They went just a short distance to rock cover and crouched behind it. They waited.

The men in the cabin heard the shots below and rushed to the door with their guns.

Devlin peered down the rocky slope. Nothing to be seen. He gritted his teeth. "I tole you boys. It's Hildy. He's spilled his guts. We got Braddock men out there. And they're carryin' rope."

The men stared at him.

Devlin talked coolly. "Max, you slip down, see if you can help Amos and Lonnie. Be smart. If they're finished, come back, take the back trail. They'll be coming up the slope."

His eyes gleamed cunningly as he considered strategy. "Might be best to separate. They won't know who to follow. Lem and Jessie, you two start now—run the back trail." He paused. "We'll meet in a week in Tombstone. Go."

Jess and Lem ran for their horses as Max started down the slope in a crouch, rifle in hand.

Devlin stood in thought. They must have caught Hildy and squeezed him, that's how the Braddock men had found the cabin. And if they knew that, they'd know about the back trail. Devlin, figuring the back trail would be covered, had used Lem and Jess for diversion. They were in a box but didn't know it—yet. They'd get caught, which might satisfy the blood lust of Braddock. It'd be Sykes runnin' these men. He knew Sykes—a bloody bounty hunter and a smart buzzard. Devlin figured he had one slim chance, a secret old Indian trail that branched off the back trail and snaked sideways

through thick pines. There he'd lay low until this rumpus was over. Devlin cursed the air blue. Hildy had put all their necks in the noose. Hildy, the weak link in the bunch.

He peered down at Max, crouched low, moving down slope to where the lookout had been perched. Devlin shrugged. Max was a goner, just like Amos and Lonnie. They were gone, otherwise they'd have put up a shout.

Devlin walked calmly to his horse, mounted, and followed the back trail for fifty yards, then turned onto the small, almost unnoticeable old trail that went into the heavily wooded land. He picked his way carefully. He had never mentioned this ancient trail to the others; it had been his secret. Devlin smiled grimly as he rode. The way you lasted in this world was to plan your backups. Especially in a business like his, where the stakes were high—your neck. The game had always been clear to Devlin: stay one step ahead of your enemy—outthink him.

Devlin listened. No firing. Not yet. But it was just a matter of time. They were finished. They'd be lucky to get shot; some would swing. He'd start a new bunch, pick men up in the territory. He cursed again. A bunch was only as strong as the weakest link, and that link had been Hildy Jones.

But how'd you build a perfect bunch?

Still, he'd known that Hildy had lusted after that floozie in Cragg. How could you keep that polecat away? Shoot him, that was how. Men like Hildy didn't want to betray you, it was their lust for women that did it.

Devlin sighed mournfully. Women were the

snares that brought some men to grief. He'd seen it again and again.

His horse picked his way carefully over the bumpy ground and through the thickly grown pines.

Then Devlin heard the shots, the sound muffled by distance.

His teeth clenched. His men were going down.

But he was safe. At least for now.

Slocum looked down at Max, lying sprawled on his face, hands stretched out. He had come down slope, as he thought, secretly, but he had stumbled into Sam's cover, and Sam had picked him off with his first shot.

Slocum felt uncomfortable. He didn't like what was happening. This was the third man who'd paid with his life for rustling Braddock. He stared at the brawny body. Rustlers didn't have much of a future.

He gazed up the slope, which curved to flat ground where the cabin nestled. Was Devlin in it? Not a chance. Not him. He was a shrewd dog and would slip out to the back trail. But Sykes would grab him, and the game would be over.

Slocum wanted it over. He had joined the Braddock bunch not to hunt rustlers, though rustlers were mangy. No, he'd joined because of Jane Bakely, a lovely girl whose land Braddock craved. In the Braddock bunch, he could help the Bakelys, get an angle on Braddock's plans.

But Sykes had locked him into this rustler jaunt, for which he had little interest. Braddock could afford to be rustled. And Sykes, jealous about Honey, figured it might be fun to put him in a frontal as-

sault, and maybe get his head blown off. Sykes was dangerous.

Slocum pulled out a cigarillo. Things were not working out as he wanted. But the rustler gang was breaking down. And once they got Devlin in the bag, Slocum felt, he could get back on target and find out what Braddock aimed to do with the Bakelys. Then he could make his move.

But they didn't have Devlin yet.

"Reckon we still got a job up there, Slocum."

Slocum looked at Sam. "Devlin won't be waiting around," Slocum said. "It's not what he does— wait."

"You figure he's run?"

Slocum nodded. "Sent these poor suckers down to give him time to get away."

"But Sykes will grab him on the back trail."

Slocum shrugged. "Maybe. They call him Slippery Devlin. Let's look."

Slocum moved up in a crouch, staying behind cover. He was sure Devlin wouldn't be in the cabin. He knew when a ship was sinking. And whoever was left of the rustler bunch would be racing the back trail—into Sykes.

They found the cabin empty and studied the markings.

Sam grinned. "As long as Devlin leaves tracks, we'll find him."

6

They followed the tracks, two horses scrambling fast and one horse moving slowly until it branched off on a small trail that looked unused and meandered toward a wooded area.

Slocum studied the tracks of the single horse. "This gent has ideas of his own." He looked at Sam and smiled. "Got to be Devlin. He'd figure a trap on the back trail and strike out on his own."

"Sounds right."

"I figure the two rustlers will ride smack into Sykes and his boys. Suppose we just tag Devlin. We're not far behind. We'll catch up."

It was an ancient Indian trail, used long ago. Slocum's keen sight studied the pines and the rocks. They rode carefully, aware that the land lent itself to ambush. But nothing happened, not for a long time. The land changed—now there were ridges

91

and gullies, more boulders, and thick shrubs. After a time they came in sight of a rock and brush cluster. Slocum felt a strong hunch that Devlin might use it to bushwhack them. It was the best position yet for that purpose. Slocum felt he could circle it.

"Why don't you set here awhile, Sam, and make a fire, so he figures we're eating and off guard. He might want to sneak bullets into us. I'm going to try and circle those rocks."

It didn't take long for him to make his circle and come behind on a crouch, gun in hand.

He was pleased to see Devlin lurking behind a boulder with his gun, trying to make up his mind about his move.

"Hold it." Slocum's voice was hard.

Devlin froze, then his head turned. He smiled painfully. "Be damned. You got behind me. How'd you do that?" He studied the big lean man coming toward him. "It's you, Slocum. What the hell are you doin', helping a buzzard like Braddock?"

"Not sure of that myself, Devlin." Slocum's face was grim. "Well, rustlin' ain't much of an occupation."

Devlin shrugged. "It's been all right—up to now."

Slocum's green eyes gleamed. "Better drop that gun."

Devlin looked thoughtful. "Not sure I want to. The game's up. Don't like the prospect of a hangin'. Nothing like dyin' quick and easy." And with a sudden move, he wheeled to shoot.

Slocum's bullet hit his gun, jerking it out of his hand.

Devlin grabbed his numb pistol hand. "Damn your hide. Why don't you kill me?"

"The order is not to kill you but make you an example of what happens if you rustle Braddock's stock."

Devlin looked grim. "One way or another, what the hell."

The shot had brought Sam with his gun, crouched and careful. At the sight of Devlin, Sam's lips twisted in a grin. "Looks like we got the big one."

Devlin shot him a cold look. "Ain't you ashamed to be workin' for Braddock?"

"Ain't you ashamed to be stealin' horses?" Sam said.

Slocum reached out a cigarillo and lit it.

Devlin watched him. "What happens now?"

"We'll take you just outside town. And when Sykes joins up with us . . ." Slocum shrugged.

Sam grinned. "They'll stretch you a bit."

Devlin looked uncomfortable and brought his hand to his neck.

Slocum said, "Let's ride."

Then they heard a voice. "Just hold it."

The voice was familiar, and Slocum recognized it before turning.

The Kid in his black mask was standing just off a big-sized boulder, lithe, lean, his gun out.

Slocum was astonished. How in hell did he happen to be here? Had they stumbled on him or had he picked them up? And what was he after?

"What's happenin' here?" The Kid's voice was casual, almost friendly.

Sam tensed. There was plenty of money on this one's head, and Sam wanted it. Trouble was, the Kid had the draw. But maybe he'd ease up, make a mistake. Sam would keep a sharp eye.

Slocum was genial. He felt kinship with the Kid, especially after the Kid had picked off that rustler aiming to steal his roan. But why in hell would he involve himself here?

"We've got Devlin, the notorious rustler," Slocum said. "We're taking him into town. Braddock wants a spectacle of what happens when you rustle his horses."

The eyes glittered behind the mask, but the Kid took his time before he spoke. "That's mighty interestin'. Reckon Devlin's been giving Braddock a big headache, stealin' his stock. Well, it don't bother me none that it bothers Braddock."

The Kid looked at Devlin, who smiled at him, pleased that the men who had him under a gun were now themselves under one. If only he could see an angle. Devlin felt his spirits begin to lift.

"Braddock's got more horses than he needs," the Kid drawled. "And I figure a man's who's got that much ought share with cowboys down on their luck."

Devlin's grin spread ear to ear. "Kid, I never heard sweeter words. Reckon you don't mind if I ride."

"On the other hand," the Kid went on with a droll tone, "rustlin' is a mangy job, and shouldn't be encouraged."

Devlin stared, then said brightly, "To tell the truth, Kid, I've become mighty discouraged about

it. Believe I learned the error of my ways."

The Kid surveyed him, and Slocum could sense his amusement. "I'm willin' for you to ride. But only if you swear to keep rustlin' Braddock."

Devlin could hardly believe his ears. But he wasn't going to question luck like this. To escape the rope—he never dreamed that. "I promise." And he moved quickly to his horse.

Slocum looked at the Kid. "I'm thinking this won't please Braddock. Not a bit."

"That makes me feel read bad." The Kid's voice dripped sarcasm.

Sam, who had been following this palaver with amazement, never once moved his eyes from the Kid. What further astonished him was that the Kid had not disarmed them. Sam's gun lay in his holster, inches from his shooting hand. He needed the Kid's attention to flicker, and he'd pick off this wild young rooster and collect that extra hundred Braddock had promised. But there was something about the Kid that seemed always alert.

Then Sam suddenly saw his moment, when the Kid glanced at Devlin as he swung over his horse. The perfect time. Sam would pick the Kid off and stop Devlin, too, not kill him. Save them both for the rope.

But just as Sam jerked his gun up, the Kid, as if he were mind-reading, made a lightning move and his gun spit fire. The bullet cracked against bone, and Sam let out a groan of pain, grabbing his shoulder as the gun fell from his hand.

Slocum didn't move.

Devlin, startled at the shot, glanced back and,

aware that all was well, put his horse into a hard gallop.

"That was a foolish move, mister," the Kid said. He looked at Slocum. "I'm glad to see you've got good sense. Now both of you—get going."

Later, as he rode, Slocum again realized that the Kid was someone to reckon with. He didn't seem overly fond of Braddock. And Braddock was out to blast his carcass too. Why? It looked like bad blood between them. The Kid had let Devlin go on the promise that he'd keep rustling Braddock, which was plenty strange. Funny, too, if you thought about it. He glanced at Sam. He'd underestimated the Kid's speed. The Kid was a real mystery. Now they'd run into Sykes and have to justify catching Devlin and then losing him—to the Masked Kid. That would make the Kid real popular with Braddock, that was for sure.

They rode toward town, and the sun was low in a red-streaked sky when they reached the creek where Sykes and his men had stopped to water their horses.

Sykes, in his yellow vest and black hat, watched them approach, and he didn't look pleased. He stared at Sam's arm, then at Slocum. "Where's Devlin?"

Slocum swung off the roan casually and brought it to the creek.

Sykes grimaced and glared at Sam. "What happened?"

Sam held his wounded arm. "We knocked off three of his men. And we had Devlin."

Sykes scowled. "*Had* him? Then what happened?"

"He got away."

Sykes, Moose, and Lefty stared at him.

"Got away?" Sykes's voice was cold.

Sam glanced at Slocum, but he seemed more interested in filling his canteen.

"It was the Masked Kid," Sam said. "Came outa nowhere. Decided to turn Devlin loose."

There was silence. Moose looked grim, watching Slocum, as if it was his fault.

Sam's broad face was impassive. "The Kid had a gun on us and told Devlin to ride. I didn't like it and tried to stop him." He held up his arm. "He did this."

Sykes's jaw was hard as he turned to Slocum. "And what about you? Why didn't *you* shoot?"

"Yeah," said Moose. "How come you let Sam take the bullet?"

Slocum's eyes narrowed. "Because it was stupid to try and beat him. Not only was he holding a gun, he's fast."

Sykes stared at Sam. "How come he got that close without you hearing him?"

Sam shrugged. "He came outa nowhere. Never heard him."

Sykes shook his head, then scratched his cheek. "Why in hell did the Kid do that for Devlin?"

Slocum smiled. "Seems he likes the idea of Devlin rustling Braddock. Thinks that Braddock should share his good fortune with some down-and-out cowboys."

The men stared at each other, then burst into laughter.

Sykes grinned. "I'm sure Braddock is goin' to enjoy hearing that he's s'posed to spread charity among poor cowboys." He looked at the horses watering. "But I don't know how Devlin's goin' to rustle. We grabbed two of his men, Lem and Jess. We hung 'em high. And you shot three. Sounds like a good day's work, even if Devlin didn't get the honors." He moved toward his horse. "Let's ride in and give Braddock the good news."

They reached the ranch in the gathering dusk. But Braddock was not there; he had gone to Black Rock on cattleman's business.

Next morning Sykes was hanging on the side of the corral fence watching Honey. She was brushing her horse, Midnight. She loved that horse, he thought, with probably the same passion she felt for men.

Sykes studied Honey's full lines, the way her riding pants hugged her buttocks, the way her breasts thrust out and jiggled with each move. A great body.

Then Sykes glowered at the thought of Slocum. She liked him, that was plenty clear. Damn Slocum. At the beginning he had felt good having Slocum in the bunch. He was a good gun, and it would make the rustling job easier. But when Sykes discovered his mistake, that Honey had met Slocum before, was sweet on him, he did the smart thing—put Slocum in the line of fire. He had hoped that he and Devlin would knock each other off. But worst luck, they were both breathing.

Sykes lit a cigarillo, his eyes still on Honey. Good thing the rustler bunch had been cracked. There was no further need for Slocum.

He thought of Braddock. What would he do when he heard about Devlin? Throw a fit. He craved to get Devlin on a hanging tree, to warn all would-be thieves. And Braddock would froth at the mouth when he heard it was the Masked Kid who had let Devlin out of the bag.

Sykes watched the smoke of his cigarillo swirl up. He wondered what in hell made Braddock so fierce about the Masked Kid. He had said it was because the Kid shot upright citizens. Sykes had to smile. Since when did Braddock give two damns about upright citizens?

No, it had to be something else. For that matter, the way he heard it from Sam, Braddock wasn't the Kid's most favorite rancher either. Like the Kid enjoyed the idea of Braddock getting his stock rustled.

Honey, aware that Sykes had been watching her, turned from currying Midnight. She glanced at his expression and came toward him. "What are you broodin' about, Sykes?"

"Broodin'?"

"Look like you lost your best horse."

Sykes clamped his jaw. "Well, we lost Devlin. That won't please your father."

She studied him. "And that's all you were thinkin'?"

He scowled. "I had other thoughts."

"Like what?"

His lips tightened. "You and Slocum. What the hell's goin' on there?"

Her lovely face froze, and her brown eyes glittered. "I do believe you're askin' a personal question, Sykes."

"Yeah, that I am."

She looked away a moment, then said, "Let me tell you, Sykes, what I do is what I do. I never yet asked anyone for permission. And I don't aim to start with you."

Sykes squirmed. She was one wild filly. Nobody put a bridle on her, not her father or anyone else. And he was trying to, because she had shown him favors. He had never met a woman like her, but then she was Braddock's filly, and he was the richest rancher around. Sykes wasn't sure how to handle her. He was used to dominating his fillies, but this one was wild. He hoped to snare her. It would be nice if he could, considering what went with her. But he'd have to play a careful hand. She was caught up by Slocum. Well, Slocum had come up fast on this turf, and he could disappear fast too. There were ways. And for Honey, a man out of sight didn't exist.

He smiled at her. "Honey, I apologize. You're a fine-spirited missy, and I admire that."

She looked mollified. "That's more like it, Sykes. You ain't a bad hombre," she said as she went toward her horse and swung over the saddle. Her grin was saucy. "When you know your place."

He watched her ride off, his eyes frosty.

In the morning, there were about ten cowboys in the chuck house, some eating, some drinking coffee. Slocum was on his second coffee, wondering if

it might be a good time to detach from Braddock, now that the back of the rustler bunch had been broken. He hated the ranch and most of the low-down men who worked there.

Of course, Devlin was running free, and Braddock, who was still off the ranch, might want nobody to leave till Devlin was hunted to ground. Braddock didn't yet know what had happened, and there had to be fireworks when he heard. Which might happen soon enough.

There were four men sitting at the next table— Lefty, Moose, Sam, and a big man called Slats. Moose was telling how they had nailed Lem and Jess and had brought them just outside of town and strung them up. Slocum found himself listening.

"Not a pretty sight, them hanging there," Lefty said. "Should scare hell outa anyone thinkin' of rustlin' Braddock."

Then Sam told how he and Slocum had shot the hell out of the three rustlers, one at a time, in front of the hideaway cabin.

"Looks like the Devlin gang is wiped out," said Slats.

"Except for Devlin hisself," said Moose, "and he'll be hotfootin' back to the hole in Kansas he came outa."

"Dunno," said Sam. "The Kid tole him he was to keep on rustlin' Braddock. That's why he helped him get off."

Moose looked mean. "Hell's goin' to break loose when Braddock hears about it." He rubbed his chin. "Damn, I'd like to get that Kid in my sights. I'd put a bullet up his tail."

"It ain't so easy," said Sam. "I thought I had him, but I didn't." He touched his bandaged arm tenderly. "He's quick."

"What the hell's he doin', ridin' around with that mask and shootin' folks?" asked Slats. "What's he after?"

"Who the hell cares. There's a fat hundred on his head, and I aim to collect it," said Moose.

"Wish you luck," said Sam, his voice a bit sarcastic.

Moose stared at him. "You weren't too bright, Sam, tryin' to hit a man who had his gun out."

Sam glowered. "He was lookin' away. Seemed the right moment."

They were silent. Then Slats said. "Now that the rustler gang is broke up, what's the next job, d'ya s'pose?"

"Probably the Bakelys," Moose said.

Slocum's attention perked up.

"That'll be a pleasure," Moose went on, grinning. "I sure like that Bakely filly, Lady Jane."

"She's a helluva looker. She sure could pleasure a man," said Slats.

Slocum turned to look at him. Slats was a heavy-shouldered cowboy with big biceps; he probably weighed two hundred and fifty pounds. He had a massive face, scarred from fights. His brown eyes were glowing as he imagined the pleasure Jane Bakely could give a cowboy like him.

"Braddock wants the water," said Lefty. "But these Bakelys are stubborn. Won't sell."

"I hear he's offered to double the price of their land."

"It's the ole lady," Moose said. "She's sentimental 'bout the land. Buried her man there and hates the idea of leavin' him."

Slats shook his head. "Braddock wants that water. He ain't goin' to be stopped by a sentimental ole lady."

"I hear old lady Bakely was ready to get out," Sam said, "till the young filly came along to live there. She's one spitfire. Just tole Mr. Braddock real sharp they didn't want his lousy money."

"She said 'lousy'?" Moose asked.

"I was there," Sam said. "Tell ya, if it hadn't been a coupla ladies, Braddock woulda cleaned them out long ago."

"So what's he goin' to do?" Moose asked. "You can't kick 'em out. Wouldn't look good for Braddock."

"I got an idea what to do," said Slats with an evil grin.

"Like what."

Slats leaned forward. "Teach the lady that it could be mighty dangerous to stay on the land. Prowlers, drifters comin' in on a dark night."

They looked at him and laughed.

"That's a good idea," said Moose. "Tell Braddock about it."

"Maybe. Or maybe just do it," said Slats. "Tell him afterward. Don't think he'd want to take the responsibility—him a big-shot citizen, and the one most to profit from it."

Moose then happened to glance at Slocum. The expression on Slocum's face hit him. Moose's smile coarsened. "What do you think of that idea, Slo-

cum? You know the filly, Jane Bakely."

Slocum's voice dripped sarcasm. "Sounds like the kind of idea that would only come to a low-down, no-account, mangy buzzard."

The men stared at him, astonished at the bite of his words. Slats, who didn't know much about Slocum, still knew when he'd been insulted. He didn't carry a gun, just two huge fists, which he figured were weapons enough.

He turned his huge body toward Slocum. "Do I understand, mister, that you'd be calling me a mangy buzzard?"

"More than that," Slocum said.

Slats exhaled heavily. "I don't like a fight so soon after eatin', but I know when I been insulted." He stood and rolled up his sleeves, revealing his huge biceps. "I'm goin' to bounce your head on the floor like a rubber ball, mister, to teach you respect."

Slocum scowled. "Just let me finish this coffee. Hate to waste a good cup."

Slocum finished his cup and then stood up and faced Slats. He was a solidly massed body of muscle and looked plenty tough. He had a thickly boned, scarred face, small eyes, a busted nose, and a heavy jaw—a man who liked fighting. He moved on the balls of his feet, surprisingly light for a big man, as he came toward Slocum, his huge fists clenched.

Slocum eased back, which made Slats grin. He rushed in, feinted, and shot a left, then followed it with a right that brushed off Slocum's shoulder. Slocum drove his right into Slat's gut.

Slocum felt the sting go up his arm. The man had a corded gut. Slats stumbled back, and as he did, he

threw a punch that caught Slocum on the cheekbone. It jolted Slocum, and he stumbled. With a
growl of pleasure Slats lunged forward, swinging at
Slocum, who dodged all but one shot, which hit his
forehead and felt like a sledgehammer. Slocum
staggered. Slats, grinning in triumph, rushed in,
swinging again, and hit Slocum's jaw hard, rocking
his head back. Slocum grabbed Slats, holding him,
waiting to clear his head. Slats swore and tried to
shake loose. Slocum held on, then suddenly let go
and, bending, swung a hard right into Slat's stomach, following it with two more rocketing punches.
A quick glance to Slat's face showed he'd been hurt.

Slats, scowling, came forward now, closing in for
a kill, ignoring Slocum's feints, and Slocum slipped
in past his guard and drove hard to the face.

Slats shook his head in fury, his nose spattering
blood. He came up blindly with cocked fists, swinging wild, but Slocum danced right and left, then
smashed to the gut again, putting his whole
shoulder behind it. His fist sank in two inches. Slats
quivered in shock, and Slocum, grabbing the moment, went for the jaw, a sledgehammer blow, putting all the power of his back muscles behind it. He
hit the solar plexus, a cracking sound, and suddenly
the small eyes in Slats's face went empty, his face
went blank, and he shook like a tree struck by lightning. Then his legs caved in and he dropped flat on
his back, lying there twitching until he went still.

The sudden end shocked the watching men.

Slocum looked at Slats sprawled on the floor,
then looked at the others. They were stunned.

"Damn, if that ain't the limit. You beat Slats," said Lefty in a wondering voice.

Slocum put his hand to his bruised cheekbone. He felt plenty racked and ruined himself. He took a couple of deep breaths. "Well, I know I've been in a fight," he said and walked toward the door.

It was early afternoon, and Sykes and some of his men were watching a cowboy trying to break a wild bronc in the corral when Braddock rode up.

He dismounted and grinned broadly at Sykes. He had known about Hildy Jones, and that Sykes had a line on Devlin's hideaway. Braddock was expecting good news.

He strode up to Sykes, who came down off the fence to meet him.

Braddock's grin was still broad. "I heard there was some neck stretching. I reckon yesterday was a good day."

"Not too bad, Mr. Braddock."

Braddock was startled. "I expected a bigger holler than that. You busted that rustling bunch of dogs, didn't you?"

Sykes smiled slowly. "I'd say that's what happened."

Braddock's grin came back. "That's fine. Strung 'em up. Left them twisting. Made a horrible example. That right?"

Sykes gazed straight at him. "We strung up some, shot some. The shootin' couldn't be avoided."

Braddock's smile faded. He didn't like the feeling he was getting. "And Devlin? You hung him, right? Where'd you leave the body?"

Sykes pulled out a cigarillo. Braddock watched with narrowed eyes.

"Well, about Devlin . . ."

Braddock's face went red. "He got away. That's what you goin' to tell me?"

Sykes bit his lip. "Not like that. We had him bagged."

Braddock came up close, his eyes glaring. "Now s'pose you tell me exactly what happened."

"They tracked him, Slocum and Sam. Caught him. And were goin' to bring him to me at the creek." He paused. "Then they lost him."

"Lost him!" Braddock was staring.

"You won't believe this, but the Kid, the Masked Kid, stepped in. Came outa nowhere, Sam said, with a gun on them. Ordered them to turn Devlin loose." Sykes stroked his chin. "Sam figured he'd try a shot at the Kid. Didn't work. Lost his shootin' arm."

Braddock looked stunned. For a few moments he digested it, then he said, "Let me get this straight. You tellin' me that they had Devlin and then this Kid came in, got the drop on your fast gun, Slocum, and that he let Devlin get away? That what you tellin' me?"

"That's it."

Braddock bared his teeth. "If that isn't the worst I ever heard." He thrust his chin pugnaciously at Sykes. "You told me Slocum was a fast gun. I paid him big money. Yet he lets a Kid get the jump on him, doesn't shoot when Sam does, and loses Devlin."

He stopped suddenly. "Why the hell did the Kid

turn Devlin loose? What's the connection?"

Sykes cleared his throat. "Sure you want to hear this, boss?"

Braddock scowled. "Hear it? Are you loco? Course I want to hear it."

"He told Devlin he'd turn him loose if he kept rustlin' Braddock."

"He what!" Braddock looked like he'd have a fit. Then he got control of himself. He surveyed the men nearby and spoke in a low voice. "Where is he? Slocum?"

"Fixin' his hurts."

"What hurts?"

"He and Slats had a knockdown fight."

Braddock slowly grinned. "Reckon Slats punched him into a pulp."

Sykes shook his head. "Well, it was Slats that called it quits."

Braddock's eyes widened. "He beat Slats? That two-hundred-and-fifty-pound ox?"

"That he did."

Braddock looked thoughtful and wondered if he might be underestimating Slocum. "Get Slocum and bring him to the house." Then, remembering how Devlin had got away, he glared at Sykes, wheeled, and strode off.

In his living room, Braddock fumed, poured whiskey, and gulped it. He thought about Devlin and the Masked Kid, and what the Kid had said: "Keep on rustlin' Braddock."

He seethed and gulped another drink.

When Sykes brought Slocum into the room, Braddock stared at the big, lean man with the cool

green eyes. Slocum's cheeks were bruised, but he didn't look like he had tangled with a 250-pound ox.

Braddock spoke in a tone softer than Sykes expected. "Must say, Slocum, I'm disappointed. Sykes told me about the way you lost Devlin. How could you let a sawed-off Kid get the jump on you?"

Slocum looked calmly at Braddock's bull-like features. "He may be sawed-off, but he's quick. And smart."

Braddock looked suddenly enraged. "I don't want to hear that stuff. He's a killer. Shootin' innocent men. And turnin' rustlers loose." He stared coldly at Slocum. "When Sam tried a shot, that gave you a chance. Why didn't you fire?"

Slocum smiled coolly. "The Kid had his gun out. It was stupid for Sam to go for a shot. I'm not stupid."

Braddock lit a cigar and stared at Sykes and Slocum. "I'm payin' you men good money, and I expect to get my money's worth. I don't think you're doin' your job."

Slocum smiled. "Well, I figure we broke this rustlin' bunch. Devlin by himself ain't goin' to do much. Maybe you don't need me anymore."

Braddock was astonished, and his jaw clamped. "Wait a minute. This job ain't over. There are two polecats out there running loose. They gotta be cut down. That's the job. You can't walk out now." His face looked grim.

Slocum stared at the big angry rancher. He's telling me I'm with him or against him, Slocum thought. Slocum was on the edge of saying he was

through anyway, then wondered if it was the right decision.

Braddock's voice was hard. "This Masked Kid. I want an all-out search on him. He's gotta go down, whatever else happens. That clear?"

Sykes nodded. "Sure, Mr. Braddock. We'll go after him. He's a dead kid." He turned to Slocum. "So what's it to be, Slocum? You ridin' with us?"

Slocum shrugged. "I'll stick. There doesn't seem much left to do." He caught the gleam of disappointment in Sykes's eyes.

But Braddock looked pleased. "I got faith in you boys. Go get 'em. Get Devlin. But I want the Kid more. String him up. We want to keep the territory clean."

As he walked into the hot sun, Slocum couldn't help but think that to keep the territory clean they needed to get rid of men like Braddock and Sykes.

As Slocum stood there thinking, Sykes came out of the big house. "Hey, Slocum."

Slocum turned to look at Sykes as he walked up close, his dark eyes cold.

"Surprises me that you wanted to quit. You knew we still had a job out there."

"Yeah, but I figured you could handle it," Slocum said. "Devlin has no backup."

"I reckon Braddock expects loyalty for his money."

"His money. He thinks about money a lot."

Sykes grinned. "Don't we all. Anyway, tomorrow, first thing, we'll go on a hunt for the Kid. Keep yourself ready."

"I'll be ready," Slocum said. "Right now, I'm riding to town."

Sykes nodded. He'd be goin' in himself later. The saloon offered men relaxation at the end of the day. He watched Slocum go for his horse and start to ride. His shrewd eyes stayed on him until he made a turn on the trail and went out of sight.

Thoughtfully, Sykes rubbed his chin. Why, he wondered, did Slocum want to walk out of the bunch? Why put distance between him and Honey? He had a lust for Honey, that was clear. That was puzzling.

Sykes had been disappointed when Braddock turned down Slocum's offer to quit. He himself had no further use for the big man from Georgia. Slocum was right, though: now that they had busted the rustler bunch, things were easier. Devlin was no hot gun, and he could be tracked by Sam.

Curious how Braddock didn't want anyone walking out on him. He liked fast gunslingers around him. No, Braddock didn't like them leaving him unless they went flat out.

Again he wondered why Slocum wanted to quit. A mystery. He'd been amused when Braddock demanded why Slocum didn't shoot at the sawed-off Kid when Sam did.

"I'm not stupid," Slocum had said. "The Kid had his gun out." It made sense.

Then Sykes thought about Honey. She had put a bad edge on him. What did she say that infuriated him? "You're not a bad hombre, long as you keep your place." What did that mean? She thought herself too good for him, that's what it meant. A filly

like that, so proud. There'd be a big kick in humbling a proud filly. But how do you do it?

Her remark was a low blow. And he'd make her pay for it. But he had to play a smart hand. It wasn't enough just to tumble her, though that prospect was exciting. Sykes's eyes glittered at the thought. But he had to keep in mind that if he really nailed her, he'd get everything that went with her, Braddock's only daughter.

The key was to get Braddock on his side. Braddock couldn't handle the gunplay needed to keep the ranch from the buzzards who always gathered at a feast—and his stock was a feast. But Braddock might have big ideas for Honey. She was the apple of his eye. And he had ambitions. Still, she did what she wanted. Sykes pondered how he could get Honey. The clearest way of all, it seemed, was to wipe out all rivals.

That meant Slocum, first of all.

She was one hot-blood, and she was unpredictable. Sykes remembered the way she had looked at Slocum. Yes, Sykes thought, the quicker he got rid of Slocum, the better.

He had to work on it.

7

The sun was midway down in a hard blue sky when
Slocum rode into town. Folks had been shopping,
picking up supplies, and loading them on wagons.
He dismounted near the general store, where he
bought some sundries. When he came out, he saw
two men come out of the saloon. They were headed
toward their horses, tied up past Laura's Cafe.
Their faces were flushed, and to Slocum they
looked like drifters. They were stubble-bearded and
wore dirty shirts and worn Levi's. They had been
drinking enough to be unsteady and high-spirited.
Slocum, walking toward the cafe himself, followed
their wavering route. Then the unpredictable happened: a young woman came out of Laura's Cafe,
talking to someone inside, and bumped one of the
unsteady cowboys. Because his balance was precari-
ous, he teetered, then went sprawling in the dust.

He lay there, sputtering curses, then turned to look at the woman.

It was Jane Bakely, Slocum noted, as he came forward. "I'm sorry," she said.

The drifter, still on the ground, said, "Why in hell don'tcha look where you're goin'?"

She flushed at his rude words.

He had ignored her apology. "What are you—a crab walkin' backwards?"

She looked at him, stony-eyed.

He got her in focus and became aware she was one very pretty girl. He got up slowly and spoke to his sidekick. "What d'ya think of this filly, Tom, knocking folks over?"

Tom grinned at the humor of it. "Coulda broke your neck, Willie. Reckon she owes you somethin'."

Jane spoke calmly. "I'm sorry I bumped you, mister. But perhaps you swilled too much."

"Oh, swilled too much." Willie showed big yellow teeth. He surveyed her rosy cheeks, her slender figure. "Tell ya what. You gimme a nice juicy kiss and we'll forget the whole thing."

Slocum moved closer, as did some folks from the cafe, aware there might be a bit of fun.

Jane Bakely gazed at Willie, more amused than insulted. "I think I'd rather kiss a mule," she said.

Willie didn't quite get the drift of her insult. But when he did, his arm shot out with unexpected speed and grabbed her, bringing her face close to his. It caught her by surprise, but not Slocum, who slipped forward quickly and with a steel grip caught Willie's encircled arm and twisted it so that Willie

faced him. Then Slocum shot a short right punch to Willie's jaw, and he fell like a log.

Tom, his sidekick, in a sudden fury at the attack, turned to Slocum, then sized up the dangerous-looking cowboy and decided on discretion. He leaned down to Willie, who looked foggy.

Slocum's voice was gentle. "You ought to take Willie on a long ride for his health."

Tom glanced again at the lean, dangerous man. "Maybe that's a good idea."

He helped Willie up, still dazed. "Let's go, Willie. This ain't much of a town. Everyone knockin' you down. Let's get the hell out."

They watched Tom help Willie stagger to his horse and push him into the saddle. Then Tom, pulling on the reins of Willie's horse, rode east, out of town.

Slocum looked at Jane. Her auburn hair glinted richly in the sun. She wore a blue shirt that hugged her breasts, and fine-fitting Levi's. The clear blue eyes in her lovely face looked at him calmly. "I suppose I should thank you."

"It was a pleasure," he said.

"I could have handled it," she said, still calm and detached.

That startled him, but he said politely, "I'm sure you could have."

They walked together on the boardwalk toward her horse.

"In a way, I was at fault," she said. "I was talking to Laura and walking out the cafe backwards."

"Willie was no gentleman," Slocum said.

"So few are." There was an edge to her voice.

Her glance seemed anything but friendly. "I'm surprised you stepped in. Didn't think you were on our side."

He frowned. "Why'd you think that?"

The blue eyes gleamed frostily. "You're riding with the Braddock bunch. That's not our side. And after what I told you about him."

They had reached her horse. "Perhaps we ought to talk," he said.

She shrugged. "Not sure there's much to say. Anyone working for Braddock is not friendly to the Bakelys."

He smiled slowly. "Don't blame you for thinkin' that. But the truth is, I'm ridin' *with* them, but not *for* them, if you get my drift."

"Not sure I do."

"I don't care much for Braddock or Sykes, as I told you. But sometimes you ride with the opposition. To help your friends."

"And how do you do that?"

"You try to learn their plans. 'Forewarned is forearmed,' as the saying goes."

A small smile creased her lips. "And have you learned anything?"

He looked grim. "They might want to scare you off the land. Funny business. A night prowler."

Her eyes narrowed. "That won't scare us. I'll be watching."

"I'm thinking of walking out on Braddock." He smiled grimly. "He warned me not to welsh on him. I could help you."

She smiled at him brilliantly. "I didn't misjudge you, Slocum, after all, You really are a friend. But I

wouldn't want you to get into trouble. Don't rush your decision. And don't worry about us. We can take care of ourselves."

He watched her supple body swing over her horse. There was something about her. She seemed unafraid of anything. She believed she could handle anything. An extraordinary young woman.

"I'll keep an eye on things," he promised.

She looked at him and suddenly blew him a kiss.

It was surprising, as was the glow it sent through him. He watched her ride, erect and lovely, and it made him think of someone, perhaps long ago, but he didn't quite know who.

He shook his head and walked toward the saloon.

After dinner that night, Braddock came out of the big white house for his whiskey and cigar. He teetered back on his chair and looked at big silver stars glittering in the sky, millions of them, stretching as far as the eye could reach.

But Braddock's mind was not on the mystery of the heavens. He was on earth and brooding on a closer mystery. The mystery of the Masked Kid. Who was he? And what the hell was he doing? He was killing picked men. Braddock had told his boys that the reason he wanted the Masked Kid wiped out was because he'd been shooting upright citizens. But in fact Braddock didn't give a damn about upright citizens; rather, he found it powerfully interesting that these particular citizens were getting clobbered.

He knew every man who'd been shot. Knew

them a long time, in fact, his memories of them going back to his youth, a time of bold and desperate actions.

He thought of himself as a young man, built like a bull, in Missouri. He thought of his wretched childhood, of Tom and Luther, his two brothers, sweating to scratch a living from their mother's parched, stony farm. Then deciding after the war to get the hell out of Missouri and go southwest. He remembered what they did to survive—rob stages. Tom got shot during a holdup outside of Twin Forks. And he lost Luther in a barroom brawl in Tucson.

That left him alone, but he felt invincible, with the bull strength of youth. He scraped out a miserable existence, mostly with his gun, and picked up with some ex-Missouri boys. Then they blundered into great luck when he ran into an old prospector who told him about the gold. It made their fortune. He thought of his sidekicks in that desperate adventure: Jared Cooper, Charley, Seth, Luke, Jim Welch. Braddock's face hardened. These men, though not all—yet, had been shot by the Masked Kid.

Why? Was it a strange coincidence? A Kid on a rampage of stage killings who happened to hit them? Or was it the finger of fate, reaching across the years? Who was the Masked Kid? A ghost out of the past, with an avenging gun? No, impossible. Just a Kid, a young stripling, who by chance had shot these particular men, men who over the years had established themselves as wealthy ranchers.

Still, the killings were enough to chill Braddock's blood.

Braddock downed more whiskey to soothe his fears. He thought about the Kid. He'd been infuriated when the Kid stepped in, turned Devlin loose, and told him to keep on rustling. Both the Kid and Devlin should have been gunned down on sight. He'd given orders. It didn't happen. But almost happened. Damn Slocum! He was the one who'd flubbed it. He should have chanced a shot when Sam did.

Braddock felt he could never rest until the Kid was deep in Boot Hill. There was something fearful as well as mysterious about this damned Kid. A ghost riding.

He had to be strung up. Braddock swore he'd ride out to see the body.

Only then would his fears disappear and he would find peace of mind.

They were going on the hunt tomorrow, a picked bunch of gunslingers. They'd get him. They had to get him. Only then would Braddock sleep well again.

He poured another drink.

Sykes pulled out a chew of tobacco and bit at it. Then he saw Moose, whom he'd been waiting for, come out of the bunkhouse, walking toward the corral with his natural swagger.

Sykes studied Moose—his husky frame, broad brutal face, washed-out gray eyes, and stubbled beard. He had picked Moose up in Tombstone with

Frankie. A gunslinger, that's all, no big brain, but ready to do his share of dirty work.

He beckoned to Moose, who came over and pulled out a cigarillo.

"Headed into town, I reckon?" Sykes said.

Moose grinned evilly. "Yeah. Goin' to liquor up and get me a piece of ass."

Sykes's mouth twisted in a sardonic smile. "Reckon we all need a touch of pleasure after a hangin'."

"Hangin' rustlers don't upset me," Moose said, grinning.

Sykes stared coldly at Moose. "Nor me." He squirted tobacco juice. "Ever think of Frank, your ole buddy?"

The look of jollity went out of Moose's face. His lips tightened as he remembered how Frank had died.

Sykes closed in. "He was your sidekick."

"Yeah, he was, Sykes. We buddied since Tombstone."

Sykes nodded. "Yeah, I figured. That's why it sorta troubled me when you did nothin' to ease your hurt after he got killed."

Moose stared, speechless.

"Yeah." Sykes looked at the distant sunlit cliffs. "I remember when Frank went down. He turned to you at the moment of dyin'. Remember?"

Moose's eyes narrowed. "I know what he told me, Sykes. Told me to kill Slocum." He threw down his cigarillo and stomped it. "And that's what I wanted. But you stopped me cold. You told me that Braddock wanted him. So I let him be."

Sykes's smile was cunning. "Sure. Braddock wanted his gun to help us break the rustler bunch. But that's done now, ain't it?"

Moose kept staring, then a light came into his eyes. "That's right. We got no more use for him." He leaned forward, his voice grating. "Never needed him, I believe."

Sykes just shrugged and kept on looking at Moose, as if waiting for something.

Moose bit his lip. "You tellin' me that Slocum's no longer off limits?"

Sykes shrugged. "If a dyin' friend told me to do something, I'd consider it a holy mission."

A slow grin spread over Moose's brutal features. "That's how I'm thinkin' about it, Sykes. A holy mission."

Sykes nodded and turned away. "Might be some fun in town tonight. See you there later."

Main Street was busy when Slocum rode into town. It was Friday, and cowboys, after a week of ridin' the range, had come in for fun and frolic. That meant liquor, gambling, and women. It meant cattle talk and gossip. Settlers buying supplies from the general store to load on their wagons.

Slocum stopped at Laura's Cafe for steak and eggs. Laura came to his table with the food. She was a buxom, well-built woman of forty, with dark brown eyes and hair going slightly gray.

"Seen Jane Bakely?" he asked.

"Not today." She smiled, aware of his interest in Jane.

He ate thoughtfully, and she watched him. "I

hear that you boys busted the Devlin bunch."

He nodded.

"But that Devlin got away."

He glanced at her. Nothing escaped a woman like Laura. In the saloon and the cafe, you heard all the happenings of a town.

"I knew Devlin," she said. "A sly, roistering rascal. Slippery as a snake." A small smile twisted her lips. "You know what they say?"

He looked up from his plate.

"They blame you for Devlin's getaway."

He just shrugged.

She leaned toward him. "I heard all about it. Then I told them you'd have to be a lamebrain to pull your gun on the Masked Kid."

He studied her. She looked like someone who learned things, who knew the territory.

"Who is this Masked Kid anyway?" he asked. "Got any idea?"

A wisp of hair had fallen in front of her brow, and she brushed it back. "It's a puzzle, isn't it? I believe he's from this territory. That something's bothering him. And he's trying to square it."

She shook her head slowly. "But who he is—that's the puzzle."

Slocum thought about it. "So you think he's trying to square something?"

"Well, he's not robbin' anyone. But he's been shootin. Who? And why's he doin' that?"

"He's got a grievance?"

"That's how I figure it."

Slocum nodded. "And Braddock's in a heavy sweat to get a rope around his neck."

"He sure is." She looked out the window at two cowboys riding past. "Some of those men who got shot were ranchers. He don't like the idea of men like that getting shot. Men like him. Makes him nervous."

"Yeah, he's plenty nervous," Slocum said, recalling Braddock's eagerness to put a price on the Kid's head.

She gazed at him. "What about Devlin? What happens now?"

"We're goin' on a search-and-lynch party tomorrow for those gents—Devlin and the Kid. Might take a few days."

She gazed at him almost reproachfully. "Are you sure you want to be in the bunch that brings down the Kid?"

He stared. "That's a strange question. The Kid's been killing."

"Not killing. He gives 'em a fair shake, I've heard. It's always a draw."

Slocum smiled. "If you're a lightning draw, it's murder, isn't it?"

She frowned. "I don't know. They don't call it murder if you get an even chance to draw your gun."

Slocum looked pensive. "Fact is, the Kid did me a favor. Shot a rustler who wanted my horse. He was goin' to shoot me, too."

She digested it, then smiled. "He did that? You see? He's not a low-down skunk. He's got class."

Slocum nodded. "He's got class, but he's not long for this world—if it goes the way Braddock wants it."

She shook her head sorrowfully and stood up to take care of another customer.

Slocum walked into the street. It was sundown, and the sky flamed red and orange. A lot of the older folks, on their wagons groaning under supplies, were heading out to their homes. As Slocum walked up the street, he heard the sound of laughter and the clink of glasses coming from the saloon. He noticed the horses, plenty of them, from Braddock's ranch.

He pushed open the batwing doors, and the smell of whiskey and tobacco rolled out at him. About ten cowboys were lined up at the bar drinking, and there were cardplayers at four tables. Some party women in short bright dresses lolled about with a few interested men.

Slocum went up to the bar and asked for whiskey. The barkeep poured a shot and left the bottle. Slocum tossed off the drink, poured another, and glanced about.

Sykes was at a table, playing poker with Braddock men. Susette, a lovely redhead, was sitting in the corner with a cowboy in a yellow shirt who looked drunk.

Nearby, at the bar, were more Braddock men, including Lefty and Moose.

Slocum, whose habit it always was to scan his surroundings with care, caught Moose looking at him; he didn't nod, just turned away. And Slocum, whose survival depended on his great instinct for danger, felt his skin prickle.

Something was different about Moose.

Slocum had caught it in his face just before turning. He looked like a man with killing on his mind. Slocum's mouth tightened. He'd always been leery of Moose since his showdown with Frank. It was why he'd kept a sharp eye on Moose, expecting him to try to back-shoot him. But after Sykes clamped down and told Moose that Braddock wanted Slocum's gun, Moose had pulled in his horns.

Now Moose was different. Slocum had read the look in his eyes. It was always the eyes that betrayed a man. For reasons unknown, Moose had again become a live gun. That didn't mean he'd meet in a one-to-one draw, though. Most likely, a man like Moose would fight dirty—that was his style.

Then Susette glanced at him, red hair, blue eyes, hefty breasts. He felt horny. But the drunk cowboy kept talking to her. She wasn't listening much. Slocum scrutinized the cowboy and decided not to push it. A drunk with a woman on his mind could be touchy and go haywire fast. Slocum wanted a quiet night, if he could get it. He glanced toward the cardplayers, and Sykes waved at him.

Slocum walked over.

"Feel like losin' money?" Sykes asked.

Slocum smiled. "Never feel like that."

Sykes laughed. "Why don't you sit in? Teach you the fine points of the game."

A player stood up. "Take this chair, Slocum. But it won't bring you luck."

Then the dark-haired cowboy sitting next to Sykes spoke up. "I don't know. Luck follows Slocum like a dog."

Slocum sat down and examined the cowboy. He looked stalwart, a gunfighter, with an almost handsome face—black eyes, smooth features, straight nose, dimpled chin. He looked easy, but Slocum sensed that he could be fast and dangerous.

"This is Johnny-O," said Sykes with a sly smile. "Just joined us."

Johnny-O smiled wickedly. "I heard of Slocum," he said, his accent Southern.

"Did you? Where was that?" Slocum's voice was genial.

"Knew a couple men in the Georgia Regulars," Johnny-O drawled. "When we talked war, they told about John Slocum, best sharpshooter in the company, knocking off bluecoats with stripes."

The men at the table looked at Slocum.

But his mind had already skidded off, the way it always did when the war came up. He remembered the shootings, the cries of pain, the wounded—all the ugly memories of war. And he remembered coming home, back to the plantation, family land for generations, to find a carpetbagger judge who dared claim it. There was a burst of rage and, when it was over, a dead judge. Slocum became a man on the run. It brought him west, where a man could live down his past. It made him the eternal drifter.

His mind came back to the game. Sykes was shuffling the cards, but he was looking thoughtful, not ready to deal. "It was a bad war, Slocum. Brother fightin' brother."

Slocum said nothing.

Sykes glanced at the other players, Lefty, Johnny-O, a local gambler named Jim, and Jeb, a

husky, scowling cowboy whose flushed whiskey face looked sour because he didn't like the way his game had been going.

"Look at the men sitting here," Sykes said. "Two Rebels and two Yanks. We're all together now. The fightin's over."

Slocum gazed at him. "A way of life is gone, Sykes."

"A way of life? Like what?"

"Beautiful women in crinolines, soft-talkin' folk. A gallant way of life is gone," Slocum said. "The world's got mean."

Sykes grinned and began to deal. "The world's always been mean, Slocum. You been seeing it through rose-colored glasses."

Slocum glanced at the bar, where Moose was watching him with pig eyes. "Yes, there's always been mean men, spoiling the life. Spoiling the earth," said Slocum.

Sykes nodded. "Look at the territory, crawling with lowlife, killers, drifters, vermin. Out to rob, rape, and kill. That's what you got crawling the territory."

"It doesn't have to be that way," Slocum said.

Johnny-O spoke in his soft drawl. "I reckon Slocum tries to do his bit."

"What's that mean?" demanded Sykes.

Johnny-O's smile was a bit strange. "Maybe he's figurin' on cleanin' up the territory."

Sykes laughed. "He'd need the biggest shovel in the world." He started to deal.

Slocum picked up his cards, then glanced at Johnny-O. "Where do you hail from?"

"Atlanta."

Slocum looked grim as he remembered how that beautiful city had been sacked.

"Johnny-O worked with me in Dodge City," said Sykes. "A handy man with a gun."

"He looks it," Slocum said.

"They tell me you pull a fast gun, Slocum," Johnny-O said politely.

"I try not to pull it," Slocum said, "unless I have to."

A mocking smile creased Sykes's lips. "Well, Johnny-O likes to pull his gun, and then a poor critter dies."

Jeb, who had lost a lot of money, mostly to Johnny-O, and didn't like him, spoke brusquely. "Hey, Sykes, I came to play cards. We're doin' a lot of bullshitting."

Sykes grinned. "Jeb was a bluebelly; he's got no sentiment. He's here to play." He glanced at the pile in front of Johnny-O. "Trouble is, he's getting bad cards."

"Rotten cards," growled Jeb, reaching for the whiskey bottle in front of him.

They began to play, and Slocum, too, got poor cards. By not playing them, he kept his losings slim. Johnny-O got good cards and played smart poker, and his winnings piled up.

As time went on, Jeb kept drinking, and his face flushed and scowled more and more. He began to watch Johnny-O as if expecting to catch him with hidden cards.

The winning cards Johnny-O got seemed too lucky, even to Slocum.

The trouble began when Jeb's cards also became good, keeping him in the pot and depleting his funds. He had started with a lot of dollars, and they were melting away.

He was a poor loser, he kept drinking, and it was pushing him to the edge.

Then the pot came when Jeb drew a full house— queens and tens. He felt his hand was unbeatable, and, determined to recover his losses, he bet everything. To his pleasure, Johnny-O stayed in all the way. The pot was huge.

In the showdown, Jeb laid out his full house with a broad smile.

Johnny-O didn't smile; he was an unsmiling man. But he showed his four deuces—the winning hand.

Jeb stared disbelievingly at the cards, his eyes glaring. Then he spit out the venomous words. "Damn your hide, you sharper, where the hell did you get those cards?"

Everyone froze.

The cardplayers stood quietly and backed away from the table.

Jeb and Johnny-O faced each other. Johnny's voice was silky. "Do I understand you? Are you impeachin' my honesty?"

Jeb's face was distorted with fury. "Listen to that shit. Nobody gets cards like yours all the time. You gotta be a sharper." He leaned forward. "We beat your ass in the war, and you keep tryin' to rob us ever since."

Johnny-O sat still. "You oughtn't to play cards, Jeb, if you don't like losin'. You're a pitiful speci-

men of a Yank." He stood up. "Why don't you pull your gun."

Jeb, too far gone to stop, slowly stood. In his time he'd shot five men, and he didn't fear this gunman. He felt he could hold his own against a top gun. But as he went for his holster he was amazed at the speed of this dark-eyed gambler whose hand movement was a blur. His gun spit fire, and Jeb felt white-hot pain in his wrist. His gun clattered to the floor.

Johnny-O didn't smile, but his dark eyes had an amused glitter. "Didn't care to take your life as well as your money."

Jeb grabbed his bleeding wrist and, suddenly sobered, realized his life had been spared. He bit his lip to say something, but nothing came out. Then he turned sharply and went for the door.

Slocum had watched Johnny-O's gun move. It had been smooth as silk, no waste motion. A tough man to face in a showdown, he thought.

Sykes stared at Johnny-O. "You're gettin' mighty soft in your old age."

Johnny-O shrugged. "I said it. I had his money. That was enough."

Sykes looked around restlessly. "Well, let's play."

"I've had enough cards." Slocum said, and he walked off toward Susette's table.

Moose stood facing out, his elbows on the bar, his small eyes shining in his broad, coarse face. He'd been drinking for hours, and it did interesting things to him. It excited his memories and gave him a feeling that he was unbeatable.

His mind worked on Frank, his companion in crime since the Dodge City days. They had gone through hell-fire together—stage robbing, rustling, gambling, drinking, and whoring.

Then, one bad day, Frankie had pulled his gun on Slocum and it had finished him. Frankie, practically a brother, was gone, leaving Moose lonely, without a real friend in the world.

And Slocum had done it.

And as Frankie lay dying, he laid a holy burden on Moose: "Kill him for me, Moose." Those were his dying words. A man worth anything took such words to heart.

In the beginning, Moose was for gunning Slocum down quick—a dark night, a bullet in the back. But Sykes had stopped him cold. And Moose couldn't cross Sykes.

So Moose had sulked, tried to conceal his feelings, and bided his time. He never smiled at Slocum; he was no hypocrite. There'd been times when he could have slipped a bullet in Slocum's back. He hadn't dared to. But now it was okay— Sykes had given the go-ahead. And in Moose's mind, Slocum was already buzzard meat. The trick was how to do it. Slocum had seen him when he came into the saloon, and Moose didn't much like Slocum's look. He'd seen that look before; it was dangerous.

Moose sneaked a glance at Slocum sitting at the card table like he hadn't a care in the world. Yet studying him, his lean square face, his powerful body, Moose felt a tremor of fear. Slocum had a deadly draw, no doubt about it.

It'd be suicide to hit him straight. Moose needed

a backup to be sure. Would Squints, one of the bunch nearby, help? He wasn't sure. Or maybe he could work alone in the black shadows outside, wait until Slocum came out to get his horse. Moose would fire quickly when Slocum swung over his saddle. Moose, imagining it, couldn't help but smile. He could see Slocum fall. And he'd realize, in his dying throes, who had done it. Because Slocum had to know in his bones that it was Moose who had marked him for killing.

And Sykes wanted it too—that made it okay. *Why* Sykes now wanted Slocum dead Moose didn't know. Was Sykes afraid that Slocum might take over the bunch as Braddock's right-hand man? Or was it Honey? Sykes was sweet on Honey, and maybe Slocum had moved in on her. Anyway, what the hell difference did it make?

The fact was, Sykes wanted Slocum dead.

And Frank wanted him dead.

And he, Moose, wanted him dead.

Moose had seen Slocum go with Susette to the upstairs rooms. He thought of Slocum there now, screwing his brains out. Well, it was a nice send-off. Just before croaking, Slocum got him a fine piece of pussy. He didn't deserve it.

Suddenly Moose was shocked to see Slocum coming down the stairs. Moose's mind had been wandering so much that he'd lost the chance to get out to the side street for an ambush. What the hell should he do? He was so primed for killing Slocum and so loaded with liquor that he had lost his natural caution. He had to stop Slocum in his tracks—shoot the bastard right in front of Sykes.

He turned quickly to Squints, who was standing next to him, and whispered, "Back me up on this."

Squints turned, puzzled. "On what?"

"I'm goin' after Slocum."

Squints scowled. "You crazy?"

There was no time; he couldn't count on Squints. He'd handle it himself.

Slocum was coming past the bar. He wasn't looking at Moose, and Moose felt suddenly that this was it. He spoke aloud. "Here comes Slocum, the big gun. A gun without bullets."

Slocum, who had expected that Moose might act soon, was still surprised. He hadn't figured that Moose would try for a direct draw. He stopped. "You talkin' about me, Moose?"

Flushed with liquor and nursing a sense of whiskey invincibility, Moose stuck out his brutal face at the man he hated. "I'm talkin' about the man who let Devlin get away."

Slocum smiled easily. "Did I hear you right?"

Moose nodded his head. "Yeah, you let a pipsqueak like the Kid outdraw you. That's what happened, ain't it?"

Slocum looked at the red-faced Moose, who was so boozed up he was dreaming he had the speed of Billy the Kid. Well, maybe he did, maybe the booze jumped up his drawing speed. The fact was, Moose had staked him out and was ready to pay him off for Frank. It was a relief to Slocum, because to keep looking for a hidden gun in the shadows could be mighty troublesome.

"Well, Moose," he said slowly, "maybe the pip-

squeak Kid did outdraw me. But I don't believe the pipsqueak Moose can do it."

The men at the bar, by this time aware of a coming showdown, had eased back, including Squints, who wanted no part of Slocum's gunplay. The space cleared around Moose and Slocum.

Slowly Moose realized what he had done, that his intake of liquor had given him false confidence, and that, with crazy conceit, he had challenged Slocum, a dangerous gunman. Moose cursed. He had been thick-headed and was on the point of death. His mind worked in a frenzy, scrambling for an escape.

Then he made his face and his voice humble. "Hey, Slocúm, don't take me serious. It was the booze talkin', not me. I'm sorry. Didn't mean to ruffle your feelin's. Wouldn't want to tangle with a man like you. It was the whiskey talkin', not me. Be a good fella and pass it by."

Slocum was startled. The whole speech was so out of character it caught him off guard. He'd been primed to go for his holster. What the hell game was Moose playing? He was an unforgiving snake, and if he didn't strike now, he'd do it later from under a rock. It was dumb to let him off the hook. But Moose had eaten humble pie in front of the men. It left Slocum puzzled.

He glanced past Moose at the mirror behind the bar. Then he stared into the pale eyes faking humility. "All right, Moose, a man smart enough to walk away sometimes lives to fight another day."

Moose flushed and clamped his teeth tight. He felt shamed to his boots, and his hatred for Slocum was like a boiling poison in his blood. He let

Slocum walk past him, then, sure he had the edge, he yelled, "Draw, you bastard!"

There was no way Slocum could pull his gun and have time to turn and shoot. Moose went for his gun. But Slocum had kept one eye in the mirror. His move was pure speed: his left hand pulled his gun, and, without turning, he twisted to shoot under his armpit, firing twice, his bullets crashing into Moose, tearing open his chest.

Moose's eyes were wide with shock at what had happened. He kept staring, then, aware that Slocum had outguessed and outgunned him, fell with a curse. He lay on the floor, twisting in agony as his heart's blood poured out. He kept staring up at Slocum.

"May you rot in hell," he whispered.

Then he died.

Slocum turned to look at the Braddock men, especially Sykes. He'd been standing at the card table to see the showdown, and now he came forward to stare at Moose. The disappointment he felt was plain to see, but he tried to hide it as he turned to Slocum.

"That was fancy shootin', Slocum. Never saw a shot like that."

"Sorry you lost one of your sharpshooters." Slocum sounded grim.

It was a queasy moment until Sykes smiled. "Not much of a shooter. Dunno what he was tryin' to do. Even if he hit you, he'd never get away with it. That was a back-shot try if I ever saw one."

"Maybe he thought he'd get away with it." Slocum's tone was ironical. He was well aware that

Moose would never have pulled his gun without an okay from Sykes.

The barkeep, who had much experience with sudden showdowns, signaled a couple of men; they grabbed Moose and carried him out the back door.

Sykes watched. Then, as Slocum sauntered for the batwing doors, he said in a low voice, "Remember, we've got a lynching party tomorrow morning."

A lynching party for the Masked Kid, Slocum thought, staring into Sykes's cold eyes. "I'll be there."

He glanced at the men at the bar. Most looked friendly, but some were stony-faced. With a casual shrug, Slocum went out into the night.

It had been a rough evening, he thought, as he rode back toward the ranch under a big moon. Its silver light made a ghostly landscape of the twisted trees, rocks, and brush. Overhead, a nighthawk soared west, and somewhere nearby a coyote howled mournfully at the moon.

His own mood, as he rode, turned a bit mournful. He wondered why. The moon cast black shadows on the giant cliffs stretching west.

He thought of Moose, a brutal dog whose life had been spent thieving and killing, like so many of the ornery men who infected the territory. It had become the refuge of jackals.

Slocum felt he lived in a world where the threat of instant death lurked everywhere—from the hostile Apaches to the desperadoes and drifters.

Sykes had him on target. There was no doubt, Slocum thought, that Sykes had built a fire under

Moose. Telling him it was now okay to put a bullet in Slocum. Sykes didn't want Honey playing games with anyone but him.

Slocum smiled. He didn't blame Sykes, if you figured what was involved. The Braddock ranch with its huge stock was worth a fortune.

Slocum's mind drifted to Honey and he shrugged. A piece of pastry, a spoiled filly, nothing compared to Jane Bakely.

Now *that* was a woman. A thoroughbred. It was in the lines of her figure, her face, her character. A woman like her seemed to grow in the West, nourished by its freedom, tempered by its hardships.

Yes, Jane Bakely was a woman without fear, who stood up to the dangers around her. And the big danger was Braddock, a hard-fisted man, a land grabber who kept a greedy eye on the Bakely place, who'd probably'd stop at nothing to get it.

That was Braddock.

And he, Slocum, found himself riding for Braddock. Tomorrow they'd be on the trail of the Masked Kid. The mysterious kid. Once they caught up with him they'd strip his mystery. Who was he? What was he doing. They'd discover his secret.

It'd be an interesting secret, Slocum felt.

He came in sight of the Braddock ranch, with its big white house gleaming in the silver moonlight.

8

Sykes looked at his tracker, Small Dog, the half-breed scout, who was studying Devlin's markings. Sykes felt irritated because this was the second day his bunch, five of them, had been on Devlin's tail without any luck. The rustler rode trickily, and, instead of streaking for distance, he kept doubling back, throwing them off.

Small Dog pointed west, a trail that led toward the Braddock and Bakely ranches. It was a surprising move.

"What the hell's he doin'?" Sykes puzzled, turning to his men seated on their sweating horses.

Slocum stroked his chin and thought about it. Not a move you'd expect. What was Devlin's intention? He knew the bunch would be after him, and his chances of escape were small. If Devlin was the man Slocum thought him to be, nothing would give

the rustler a bigger charge than to pay Braddock off for killing his comrades. Braddock didn't ride in a posse. If Devlin got hold of Braddock, he could bargain for his life.

Sykes looked at his men. "He seems to be ridin' into the lion's mouth."

Johnny-O looked thoughtful. "Maybe he figures it's the last place to look for him."

Sykes looked at Lefty and Squints. "Any ideas?"

"Sounds crazy," said Lefty.

Sykes looked at Slocum. "What do you think?"

"Might be goin' after Braddock," Slocum suggested.

Sykes thought about it. "Why the hell would he do that? Damn his hide. You'd think he'd try to run for it."

Slocum put a hand on the roan's sweaty haunches. "Maybe he figured he'd never make it if he ran. So he decided to sneak back and take Braddock with him, a payoff for what happened to his boys. Or maybe he figured he could bargain for his life if he got hold of Braddock."

Sykes pulled out a tobacco chew and bit it thoughtfully. That made sense. Devlin would pull a stunt like that. If that was so . . . Sykes licked his lips. To save Braddock's hide would give him a lot of points in his game for snaring Honey.

He looked at his men. "Well," he growled, "let's trip him. We'd better go lickety-split for the ranch."

They rode hard and fast and stopped once to check the droppings of his horse. Small Dog said, "Warm."

Sykes grinned. They'd be in time. Nothing would

please him more than to nail Devlin just when he had Braddock under the gun.

Some hours before, Devlin, looking down from a high rise, had seen the Sykes bunch snaking through a thicket. He'd been expecting them, and now he had to make his move. He had never figured on getting away, not from a vengeful bastard like Braddock.

His bunch would dog him till they trapped him, then they'd string him up without mercy. He'd end up dead, like his boys.

But there was an angle. The gunslingers were out hunting him, and back at the ranch, Braddock sat unprotected.

Devlin smiled grimly. Maybe his life was forfeit, but he wouldn't sell it cheap. There were ways. If he got hold of Braddock, he'd have good cards to play. That's when he decided to double back and go for the ranch.

It was midday, and the ranch looked quiet to Devlin. Most of the cowboys were riding the range. A couple of wranglers had been lounging around the corral, and now they were walking toward the bunkhouse.

Devlin had been watching the big white house through his field glasses from a stand of cottonwoods north of the ranch. He'd seen no sign of Braddock, and he was ready to go in, bold as brass.

Then the door of the house opened and Braddock's filly, Honey, came out. He watched her walk to a pinto, mount up, and take the trail north.

A fine piece of luck, he thought, moving quickly

back and hiding himself, his mind working with feverish speed. She'd be riding into his noose. Honey was a powerful bargaining chip. If he grabbed her, he could use her like a gun aimed at Braddock's head. They wouldn't dare touch him.

She went past him on a canter toward wooded terrain, and he mounted up and followed. After a while he put his horse into a gallop, and finally, when she heard him, she turned to look. She didn't seem alarmed, just curious.

He brought his horse abreast and smiled. It was easy to do, because she was one fine looker. "Hello. You'd be the Braddock filly. Honey."

She pulled up her horse and nodded. "And who are you?"

"Devlin's the name."

Her pretty mouth firmed, then she scowled. "Devlin? The rustler? Thought they had strung you up by now."

He grinned fiendishly and put a hand to his neck. "Not yet, Honey. And don't rush it. I'm hopin' maybe you'd be willin' to help."

"What do you mean, help? You're a rustler. That's a dirty business. You pay a high price for that." She stared at him curiously. "What are you doin' round here? Mighty dangerous country for you."

He rubbed his stubbled chin. "I was lookin' for your pa. Hopin' to persuade him to call off his dogs."

She smiled. "You don't know my father. How were you goin' to persuade him?"

"Well, I was hopin' to put a gun on him and tell

him it might be worth his life to call off his dogs."

She was looking at him wide-eyed.

He went on. "But since I never did see him, but did see you, I figured you might put in a word for me."

As his words sank into her mind, she laughed. "What makes you think Dad would listen to me? You must be funnin'."

"No, I'm not. He'll listen. Don't worry. You just ride along with me and you'll find out."

She stared at him, almost uncomprehending. "Are you loco? I'm not goin' to ride with you."

He had to admire her gumption. He jerked his gun out. "Reckon you better ride with me. Or your dad will find he's lost his only daughter."

Her nerves quivered. In a perverse way the situation appealed to her: a desperate gunslinger, her life in danger. Someone was going to get hurt.

"What do you aim to do?" she asked.

"Get word to your dad that if he don't call off his dogs something bad is gonna happen to the apple of his eye."

She smiled a secret smile. "All right. I'll ride with you. But I don't mind saying I think you'll end up at the end of a rope anyway you look at it."

He looked at her pleasantly. She was good stuff. "Maybe you're right. I do see a rope in my future. So you realize I've got nothin' to lose. Just stay nice and easy. Don't do anything foolish. Stick close to me."

Suddenly she glanced into the distance. "I'll stick close, but I don't think you've got a lot of time."

His head jerked around. They'd been spotted.

Six horsemen, about three-quarters of a mile away, were riding furiously toward them. Damn, it was the Sykes bunch. He hadn't expected them to be that close. He stared at the surrounding terrain. The Bakely land, hilly and wooded, might be a place to hole up. And he had the girl as hostage.

He turned to her, his eyes hard. "Stick with me, and keep up. Do as I say and you won't get hurt. But if you cross me, this'll be your last day. I've got nothin' to lose."

She stared into his eyes. "I don't think you'd shoot a woman."

"Don't try me," he warned. "Now move." He struck the haunches of her pinto and they raced toward the brush.

For the next hour Devlin did a few tricks, doubling back on his tracks twice, and he managed to shake the pursuing bunch. It gave him breathing space, time to think about the girl.

When they reached a clear spot in the brush, they dismounted. He stared at her. "Well, you're a fine-looking filly."

Her brown eyes gleamed. She saw him as a man who'd be dead in hours. He was desperate, and ready for desperate things. She found that exciting. She knew Devlin to be a clever rustler who had bedeviled her father's herds. And she knew that his bunch had been busted. Most men would have tried to escape—there was always a slim chance. But this Devlin, bold and bad, instead of running, did the opposite—he attacked. He was ready to grab her father and bargain for his freedom. He had *her* now.

Whatever would happen, he was a goner, she was sure of it.

She looked at his face. Rugged, strong, with an easy smile. Soon he'd be dead. Hanged. She felt a perverse compassion for him.

He'd been watching her, and picked up on her interest. Her face revealed her feelings. "You think I'm finished?" he asked.

"What do you think?"

He grinned. "Well, I've got you. Nobody's goin' to hit me while I've got you."

"But you wouldn't hurt me, would you?" She was smiling at him.

His eyes went stony. "Don't know what I'll do till the time comes."

She continued to smile. "No, I don't see you as a man who'd hurt me."

He bit his lip. "I don't want to. But I aim to get out of here with a whole skin."

She said nothing, but her eyes had a strange glint.

"I know what you're thinkin'," he said. "That it won't happen."

"That's what I'm thinking."

He studied her fine auburn hair glowing in the sun, her breasts, her body, her eyes. "A beautiful filly," he said.

Her deep brown eyes held boldly on him. She felt a curious surge of feelings, because he was going to die. The idea of being intimate with him excited her strangely. A crazy feeling—it was a mix of pity, fascination, and desire.

"Are you a talker or a taker?" she asked.

"Meaning what?"

"I mean do you go on talking?"

His eyes opened. "Come here." His voice was hoarse. She sauntered over to him and he put his hands on her rounded hips. She was looking at him with bold glowing eyes. She was a ripe beauty if he ever saw one. His hands went over her body, her breasts, her buttocks.

Suddenly she put her hands on his face and kissed him. He was astonished at her passion. He had thought at first she might be faking it so he'd do her no violence. But the way she kissed—that wasn't fake, it was real. Somehow, strangely, she found him an excitement. He felt the pressure of time.

His body suddenly mobilized for sex. She pulled at his shirt, and he opened her blouse. He gazed at her round, full, milk-white breasts, the pink nipples. He bent to them. She pulled him tight.

Within minutes they were naked on the grass. Her hands and mouth were all over him. He caressed the silk of her body. Her hand went down to his maleness. She brought him to her, felt his strength. He sighed as he sank into her silky softness.

Then, aware he was teetering on the edge of eternity, that this might be his last earthly embrace, his body surged against her and, in a fever of violence, he drove until the final scalding moment of release. She grabbed his body, clenched him, let out a slow moan of pleasure.

Afterward, when they had dressed, she smiled at

her wild thought: the condemned man ate a hearty last meal.

But he was looking at a hawk that had swooped down on a smaller bird.

It seemed to him a rotten omen.

Small Dog, who had been tracking Devlin, held up his hand and reined in his mustang. Sykes and the riders behind him came to a halt with a creaking of saddles.

"He's holed up in there, with the lady," Small Dog said.

Sykes looked at the tracks of two horses that went into the dense brush. Devlin and Honey in there? How long had they been there? It wouldn't be easy to ride into that without running into a fusillade if Devlin had set an ambush, Sykes thought.

Would Devlin make a stand here?

Slocum watched Sykes take off his beat-up black hat and scratch his head.

Slocum almost felt amused at the turn of events. Foxy Devlin had grabbed Honey, the daughter of his enemy, and holed up with her in the brush. A stalemate? Did Devlin have the winning card?

Sykes turned. "I think we can box him. Right, Slocum?" He held out his field glasses to Slocum, who studied the land. It could be circled. But what was the point?

Sykes didn't wait for Slocum's opinion. "Lefty and Squints, you two circle that brush and hold the ground. We'll hit him from the front. Box the buzzard."

The two men nodded and started to ride.

Sykes turned with a satisfied smile. "We'll nail him to a tree. We'll box him in."

"Then what?" Slocum asked.

Sykes turned slowly to stare. "What the hell do you mean?"

"He's got Honey. He's going to use her to save his skin."

Sykes scowled. "How's he goin' to do that?"

"He'll threaten her if we move in on him."

Sykes thought about it. "Damn. That's it. He'd hurt her to save his neck."

Slocum grinned. "A man like Devlin? He wouldn't hesitate a moment."

Sykes nodded. "He's low enough."

"A man can be low if his life's on the line. And he's got the girl."

Sykes pondered this, and looked again at the brush. "The trick is to get near him and pick him off before he can hurt the girl."

Slocum smiled. "That's the trick."

To pass the time while Lefty and Squints got into position, Sykes studied the land, the dense brush, the thin trail into it. Off to the left there was a hill. A fine spot for observation. Sykes pulled out a chew, took a bite off it, then turned to Slocum. "And you thought he was goin' for Braddock."

"He grabbed what he could. And if you think of it, he's got an ace in the hole with Honey."

Sykes looked furious. "The only hole he's got is the one he'll get in Boot Hill," he snarled. Devlin and Honey alone together made him nervous. He knew something of Honey's hoydenish nature. She was capable of anything. Jealousy spurred him.

"That Devlin is one low-down dog," he muttered. "And I don't want him abusing Honey. We'll go in there, Slocum."

They started to move slowly through thick brush, scattered rocks, small twisted trees. Finally they came to a split in the trail. "You take the right," Sykes said. "If you spot Devlin, fire three shots. I'll go left."

Slocum rode into the thick brush, dismounted, and moved forward in a crouch. Just before entering the thicket he glanced back. Sykes sat on his horse, waiting. Slocum smiled grimly. Like many men, he wanted the other hombre to pull the chestnuts from the fire.

After a lot of patient, soundless crawling Slocum found his quarry. Through a clearing, he could see them. Honey close to Devlin, looking more like his lover than his victim. Slocum grinned. Sykes's worst fears had probably been realized.

Devlin had nothing to lose, so he had decided to taste a piece of Honey. But the poor sucker, caught by her, had lost the edge he needed to survive. Slocum's gun was out, and with an easy shot he could put Devlin away. But they wanted him whole for hanging, and somehow Slocum didn't much care to be the one to finish the rustler off.

"Don't move, Devlin," he warned, stepping out.

Devlin cursed and froze. He recognized Slocum's voice and knew the game was up.

"Throw your gun," Slocum said.

Devlin threw his gun and turned around.

Honey smiled. "So it's you, Slocum. And where's my big hero, Sykes?"

"He'll be here, to make the big noise," Devlin said.

Slocum fired three shots to bring up Sykes and the others.

Lefty and Squints, who'd been lurking in brush nearby, waiting to make a move, now came riding out.

Lefty grinned. "Devlin, looks like your days are coming to a sudden end."

"Yeah," said Squints, staring at what he figured was a dead man. "You're gonna croak because of a pain in the neck."

Now Sykes came riding forward and swung off his saddle. He scowled at Devlin, then at Honey. "Did this skunk do anything he shouldn't have? Tell me the truth, Honey." His hand gripped his gun. "'Cause if he did, I'm going to subtract his dick before he swings."

Honey stared hard at him, her face calm. "I wouldn't do a thing like that to a coyote," she said. "And I don't expect you to."

Sykes turned to Small Dog. "Take her back."

Honey's face hardened. She looked at Devlin a long moment, but her face didn't reveal what had passed between them.

Sykes waited until she and Small Dog had gone, then turned to Lefty. "Tie his hands."

Lefty pulled a thong from his pocket and tied Devlin's hands behind his back.

Sykes pointed to a sturdy tree nearby. "That's a good one for hanging. Put him in the saddle."

Squints and Lefty lifted Devlin into the saddle.

"The rope," said Sykes, staring hard at Devlin.

Lefty pulled the rope hanging from his saddle horn. He deftly made a noose, then threw it over Devlin's neck.

Sykes slowly pulled out his tobacco chew and bit into it, his eyes never leaving Devlin. "End of your trail, cowboy."

Devlin just grinned. "Everyone's trail ends. I don't care."

Sykes looked disappointed, as if he expected him to break. "Well," he said grudgingly, "you got guts. Gotta hand it to you." He turned, as if trying to delay the last moment. "What do you think, Slocum?"

Slocum, who didn't like any of it, just shrugged. "He's got guts, but he wasn't smart."

Devlin scowled. "What's that mean? Don't insult me in my last minute, Slocum."

"You didn't have to rustle. With your brains, you could've done better," Slocum said.

"Got no regrets," Devlin said slowly. Then he grinned, looking at Sykes, thinking that he'd just had his woman. "I had a good run."

Sykes, as if reading this, gritted his teeth. "Say your prayers, Devlin."

"Naw, just go ahead."

Sykes nodded to Lefty, who struck the haunches of the horse, starting it forward. Devlin was pulled from the saddle and swung in the air for a moment. A rifle shot cracked and the rope split.

They all stared up the hill. There was the Masked Kid, holding his rifle. He had fired the shot. The

men scrambled for cover, but the Kid didn't shoot again, he just watched. Devlin, who had dropped from the tree looked up and began to run. Sykes fired twice. Devlin stumbled and fell. He lay there on his back, breathing heavily, then grinned up at the Kid, his eyes shining with gratitude.

"Always hated hanging," he muttered. "Thanks."

He closed his eyes and died.

The Masked Kid now disappeared over the rise.

"Let's get him," Sykes yelled. "We'll hang him instead!"

They scrambled for their horses.

Sykes, staring at the rise, dug his spurs into his horse, jumping him forward. "Come on," he yelled. "We'll never get a shot this good at the Kid."

Under the copper sky they raced their horses up the sunbaked slope. They found the Kid's marks and began to track, but it wasn't easy. He led them a twisting trail through tangled brush, trees, and rocks into the valley.

After relentless tracking, they split up and finally bottled him against a cliff. Lefty shot his horse, and the Kid jumped clear, but he stumbled on a hidden rock and tumbled awkwardly, breaking his fall to the ground with both hands.

Sykes came at him, firing two shots to keep him pinned.

The Kid froze. The men jumped from their horses and came toward him.

"Throw your gun and get up," ordered Sykes.

The Kid tossed his gun and slowly got up, dusting his shirt, looking at them through his mask.

Lefty jumped for the gun and grinned widely.

"Well, Kid, we've got you," Sykes exulted. He studied the slender young man standing proud, fearless.

Sykes lifted a cigarillo from his chest pocket and deliberately struck a lucifer. His men watched him. "You sure can shoot, Kid. That was a nice trick shot, cutting Devlin down." He shook his head. "But it was wasted. Forced me to kill him on the run, instead of stringing him up."

He glanced around. "But we got you, a consolation prize. And I'm afraid nobody's goin' to do that for you."

Slocum, puzzled, kept staring at the Kid. This was the closest he'd ever gotten to the mysterious cowboy, and something about him was familiar. What was it? Like someone he knew. It was baffling.

Sykes turned to Lefty. "The rope."

Lefty's scarred face crinkled in a ferocious grin. "We got cheated of one hangin'. Nobody's goin' to cheat us on this one. Right, Sykes?"

The Kid stood still, unafraid. He glanced at Slocum. The cool blue eyes behind the mask hit Slocum strangely. Was it an appeal? Slocum thought of what the Kid's gun had done for him—it had saved his carcass twice, and saved his horse.

Slocum realized he was not going to let this mean bunch do a lynch job.

They were looking at the Kid the way a coyote looks at a rabbit.

"I figure you're wrong, Lefty," Slocum said.

Lefty turned, startled, to look at Slocum's pistol.

"What's that?" demanded Sykes, not sure he had heard clearly.

"I figure you're goin' to get cheated of a hanging," Slocum said cheerfully.

"What's that mean?" Sykes said.

"I'm taking the Kid. Drop your guns."

They stared, icy-eyed.

"You gone loco, Slocum?" Sykes demanded.

"Maybe. Again, toss your guns."

Lefty, his scarred face grinning hideously, hating to miss another lynching, carelessly brought out his gun as if to toss it, but instead he turned up the barrel to shoot. Slocum fired, his bullet breaking the bones in Lefty's hand. Lefty howled and dropped his gun.

Slocum's cool gaze went to the others. They all pitched their guns.

He motioned to the Kid to pick them up.

"Give 'em here," Slocum said. He dropped them in his saddlebag.

"Take Lefty's horse," he told the Kid.

Not wasting a moment, the Kid slipped over the sorrel.

Sykes was staring at Slocum, almost in disbelief. "Why are you doin' this crazy thing? You don't even know the Kid."

"What the hell, Sykes. A good deed in a naughty world."

"Braddock will never let up on you."

Slocum grinned. "That should be fun." He pointed east, and the Kid started to ride.

Slocum whirled the roan after him. "Don't follow us," he warned, his voice grim. "The next shot will be fatal."

9

As they rode east through the valley, Slocum turned to make sure it was clear. When they came to a basin with a shelving rock, the Masked Kid pulled on his reins.

"All right, Slocum. I thank you for all that. We can say good-bye here."

Slocum stared. "I don't think so. They're goin' back to the ranch to get guns, and then they'll come hunting us hot and heavy. We might need each other."

The Kid stroked his chin. "Give me a gun, Slocum."

"Not just yet. I'm not sure it's safe. You just might blow my tail off."

The Kid, who edged back, as if to keep distance, shook his head. "Why would I do that?"

Slocum measured him. "You shot the hell out of four men."

The Kid's jaw tightened. "They deserved to be shot. Like dogs. They were rotten."

His voice, under the charge of feelings, cracked and went high. Something in it struck a chord in Slocum. He looked sharply at the Kid—the slender, supple body, the blue eyes—and a strange idea hit him.

"Give me a gun, Slocum," he urged, his voice back in low key now, as if aware he might have revealed something.

"I'll do that, just after you drop the mask," Slocum said.

There was a long silence. An eagle soared overhead, headed for the distant crags, picking up the golden light of the slanting sun.

"I'm not goin' to do that, mister," the Kid said.

"Oh, yes, you are." Slocum's voice was cool.

The Kid muttered under his breath, then wheeled the sorrel and started to gallop.

Slocum, with a shake of his head, put the roan after him. Somehow the Kid made the sorrel put out its best, and they went thundering down the trail, with the roan catching up slowly. Then Slocum jumped, pulling the Kid off his horse. They tumbled on the soft earth, but even before he hit the ground with the Kid, Slocum's suspicions were confirmed. The body he was holding wasn't that of a young man. A firm body, yes, but it was female. A slender young woman, strapped under a tight vest to conceal her curves. And those eyes could belong to just one young woman.

He held the struggling arms and lifted the black mask.

It was Jane Bakely.

Her hat had come off, and her auburn hair was tightly bound.

So it was Jane.

That was the mystery of the Kid. No wonder Slocum had good feelings about him, that is, *her*. The elegant touch, the nice way she handled herself.

Somehow she had learned to talk at the lower end of her voice. The voice never had been a deep male voice, but it could belong to a young man, which you'd think she was if you didn't look close.

But the way she pulled a gun, what about that? She had speed and accuracy. She must have practiced shooting endlessly to get the speed and aim. Must have been driven by demons to get so fast, to masquerade. And for what? To kill!

What drove her?

"I reckon you've got plenty of reasons for doing all this. For killing those ranchers."

"Reasons enough," she said harshly.

"And what would they be?

"Braddock knows the reasons. Why do you suppose he sent his dogs after me?"

Slocum walked to his roan, pulled a whiskey bottle from the saddlebag, poured a bit into a tin cup, and held it out.

"Suppose you tell me."

The sky was a great glow of red when Braddock, loafing in front of the white house, saw the riders coming toward the ranch. Honey and Small Dog

were out in front, but riding hard behind them were
Sykes and his boys. Braddock scowled, not liking
the look of it. What in hell was Honey doing with
them?

Things were getting trickier each day, it seemed
to him.

He turned to look at the land beyond the corrals,
his land, smooth, undulating, richly nourished. He
looked at his horses and cattle stretching out to the
horizon.

The riders came up in a clatter, but only Sykes
and Honey came toward him.

Braddock scowled. He didn't like it at all.

"What the hell is goin' on?" he demanded of
Sykes.

Sykes wiped his mouth. "Devlin is dead."

Braddock looked bewildered. From the way they
had come on, he was expecting bad news.

"Dead." He smiled maliciously. "So we finally
caught up with that buzzard. Nice work, Sykes. You
strung him up? A lesson for rustlers."

"Had to shoot him, boss."

Braddock looked mean. "I told you to *hang*
him."

Sykes pulled out a cigarillo. "I had him on a
rope, but he got shot down."

"Shot down. Who the hell did that?"

"The Kid."

Braddock cursed softly. "Again, that damned
Kid." His gaze turned to Honey. "What are you
doing with this group?"

She smiled broadly. "They saved me from Dev-

lin. He came here on the sly, lookin' for you. Was goin' to trade his life for yours. But you weren't here. I happened to ride out, and he picked me up instead."

She fixed her shirt modestly. "He was goin' to sell me for his life. But the boys came down on him like a pack of wolves. They had him primed for a tree . . ." She stopped.

Braddock stared hard at her, then flushed. He knew his daughter. He had been about to demand if Devlin had tried anything funny. But the buzzard was dead. Nothing could be done about it.

He looked at the sun-reddened sky. "And the Kid. Dead too?"

Sykes looked at the ground. "Oh, we grabbed him, all right. Now you won't believe this, boss."

"Spit it out."

"Slocum turned on us."

"Slocum!"

"Just cool as a coyote. He suddenly turned on us. Took our guns." Sykes cleared his throat. "And went off with the Kid."

Braddock looked like he couldn't make head or tail of it. "Went off with . . . Why the hell did he do that?"

Sykes shrugged. "A mystery. Last thing I'd expect."

"Damn his rotten, treacherous hide. How in hell did he get your guns, all of you?"

Sykes sounded apologetic. "Didn't expect him to pull a stunt like that, Mr. Braddock. But Lefty tried. Got his hand shot to pieces."

"You all shoulda tried," Braddock snarled.

He was silent, thinking about it, and the more he thought, the redder his face got. His voice was choked with anger when he spoke. "Sykes, get yourself some guns and go after them. Both of them. Track 'em down wherever they go, and hang 'em from the highest tree. Don't come back until it's done. Now go."

Honey stared at her father. She'd never seen him in such a rage.

Or was it fear?

Jane took the cup of whiskey and sipped at it, her blue eyes brooding. She sat on a flat rock facing the faraway rugged cliffs. It seemed to Slocum, who was sitting on a mound opposite, that something inside her was seething, craving to break out.

"My father was a miner," she started. "He struggled for years, until finally he made a lucky strike. For eight months he scraped a lost mine pocket, slowly building a prize gold hoard.

"'We're goin' to be rich folks, Janie,' he told me. I was a young girl, more of a tomboy, and that didn't mean much to me. My mother was dead. Dad taught me things, like how to ride and shoot.

"We were headed for Dawson with the hoard and stayed in a hillside cabin. One day, on the trail nearby, we ran across a young man who'd been hurt —thrown from his horse, he said. We brought him to the cabin and fixed him up. He stayed two days, during which he became curious about Dad's mining stuff. Then he left.

"The next day, four men rode toward the cabin. Dad studied them, then opened a secret cellar door. He told me to go down, and no matter what happened, not to come up.

"They came in the cabin, four men, soiled drifters. Peering from a crack in the cellar door, I could see their faces.

" 'Well, old-timer,' one of them said, 'we're thinkin' of goin' down the mine to try our luck.'

" 'That's what you need, plenty of luck. And hard work,' said Dad.

" 'We heard you been lucky. Like to see what the nuggets look like. Not bad, I hear.'

" 'Where'd you hear that?'

" 'Friend of ours, Jared Cooper.'

" 'Yes, he's been here. Surprised he told you. Who are you? What's your name?' asks Dad.

" 'Braddock. Not that it's goin' to make a difference.'

"The men laughed, thinking it a joke. Braddock, grinning, turned to them. 'Meet the boys. Jim Welch, Charley Amis, Seth William, Luke Smith. Now that we're all friends, we might look at the nuggets.'

" 'I don't think so,' said Dad. 'I got it by the sweat of my brow.'

"Braddock laughed. 'Some get gold by the sweat of their brow. Others get it by the sweat of somebody else's brow.'

"Again the men laughed harshly, enjoying the joke. They looked dirty, mangy, and bad. I was fifteen.

"'I suppose that's funny,' Dad said.

"'Not that funny,' said Braddock.

"Then Dad probably felt he was in a bad spot. He'd been a good Samaritan for a man called Jared, and this was his payment for it. Probably he wanted to be sure nothing happened to me. So he said, 'All right, I'll show you. You can dig and get them too. Sweat of your brow.'

"'Men do a lot of diggin' and just get dirt for their pains,' said Luke Smith.

"'Let's see your stuff, old man,' said Charley Amis.

"Dad showed them his hoard.

"Braddock whistled. 'Gold is a beautiful sight.'

"They were all staring at the gold, and I'd never seen greed before. A terrible thing to see. Their faces were printed on my mind.

"Then Braddock said, 'Old-timer, I hate to do this after your hard work, but we need a stake. We're at the start of things, and it looks like you're at the end.'

"'All right,' said Dad. 'Take the gold and go.'

"Braddock smiled. 'That's mighty generous. We'll do that.' He turned to his men. 'Get it together, fellas.'

"Then Braddock said, 'Mighty obliged, mister. Charley, we don't want this to get around. Take care of our friend.'

"I heard two shots and almost jumped out of my skin.

"'He's finished, let's go.'

"'Isn't there s'posed to be a kid?' said one voice.

"'The kid's not here,' said someone. 'Let's get the hell out.'

"I heard their horses.

"I waited for Dad to say something. Then I heard his moan. I pushed open the door. He was lying on the floor, bleeding. He looked at me. I threw myself on him, sobbing frantically.

"'Go to your Aunt Amy in Red River, she'll take care of you,' he said.

"I just sobbed.

"Then he fixed his eyes on me, a terrible gaze, and said, 'Pay them back, Jane. You can do it.'

"'If it's the last thing I ever do,' I swore.

"I buried him the next day. Over his grave I swore a mighty oath—to find those men and shoot them down like dogs. Their names were burned in my brain: Braddock, Jared Cooper, Charley Amis, Seth Williams, Luke Smith, Jim Welch."

By this time Jane Bakely had finished the whiskey in her cup, and she held it out for more.

Her blue eyes gazed at the sky at sundown, a great smear of red. "I lived with my Aunt Amy for years in Red River. You'll never know how I worked to avenge my father. I learned the fine art of shooting from a great gunfighter. I practiced and practiced. I had an eye; I was a natural. And I never stopped searching for Braddock.

"A little while back, my Aunt Martha wrote me from Cragg City that a man named Braddock had taken the Prescott ranch not far from her place, that he was making an offer for her land.

"Braddock!"

"Would it be the Braddock I'd been searching for? I came as fast as I could."

She had stopped looking at the horizon, remembering the past. She turned to Slocum and stared hard into his eyes. "I'll tell you this, Slocum—the Hand of God works in mysterious ways."

10

Slocum had listened riveted, powerfully moved by her story. What had happened had seared her mind, to be remembered always. She told it straight, without self-pity, but the pain lived in her eyes.

She looked at him. "They bought land with gold bought in blood. Gold wrenched with sweat from the ground by my father. They became rich ranchers. And all have paid in blood."

Her blue eyes flashed. "I shot them like dogs. Oh, I gave them more than they gave my father— the chance to draw. But I made sure they knew, at the moment of dying, it was my father striking from his grave. All of them are gone. All but Braddock."

She paused, and he wondered if she had finished. But she hadn't.

Her voice was soft. "Only Braddock is left. The worst one. And I wanted him last. He's wondering

who the Masked Kid is. I know this Braddock. He's got ice in his belly. He's having nightmares. He thought he had everything, but now he knows there's an avenger killing his fellow thieves."

Hell has no fury like the revenge of a woman, Slocum thought. Trouble was, Braddock's bunch almost had the Kid on a lynch tree, just a hairbreadth away.

Slocum said, "Braddock's been nervous about you, all right. You've got him crawling in his skin. Each man in his old gang has been chopped down. Must drive him crazy, trying to figure it out. Why them? Who's doin' it? He's goin' to come at us hard."

"After *us*?" she said tenderly. "You saved my life."

She stood and came toward him, leaning against his chest. It was a tender act, and though he felt desire, it seemed the wrong moment. But would there be a right moment? There might not.

He looked at her lovely face, distorted with the memory of the time she had lost her father.

No, the time was not now.

Sykes walked to his men. "Get yourselves ready. I've got something else to say to Mr. Braddock."

As the men went off, Braddock turned, scowling. "At a time like this, it's gotta be something mighty important."

Sykes nodded. "Mr. Braddock." He cleared his throat. "I know this ain't the right time, but there's something I gotta get clear."

Braddock stared hard.

Sykes smiled suddenly. "It's no secret, Mr. Braddock, the way I feel about your girl, Honey. The way I see it, it would be real nice if we could get together." He grinned. "She's of an age to settle down. Needs a red-blooded man to tame her wild ways."

Again he cleared his throat. "You need a good right hand to help keep the thieves out and handle your stock. And I gotta say you ain't goin' to find anyone better'n me."

Sykes patted his gunbelt. He felt he had made a good case, but the look in Braddock's eyes was unreadable. He wondered what the crafty bastard was thinking. He always figured Braddock was a four-flusher, a man who tricked his way to money and power. He had once asked Braddock how he made his stake. "Hard work and luck in the mines," Braddock had said, and the way he said it was funny. Sykes didn't believe him. He was not a patient mining type.

Braddock, on his side, was thinking hard. He was thinking that the insolence of this coyote was hard to believe. Where'd he get the balls to dream he could get Honey? *Marry* her, by God!

For Honey, Braddock had always had in mind one of the rich rancher sons in the high country. And here comes this hired gun, bustin' out of his britches, thinking he deserved to hitch up with his only daughter. Braddock would no sooner give his girl to this gunslinger than he would to an ape.

Braddock's pulse beat dangerously. He had to control himself or this pig Sykes would pick up his

thoughts. And damn, right now he needed Sykes. To get rid of those two devils.

That Masked Kid was like some avenging demon who had come out of the past with a killing gun.

Braddock felt the ice of fear in his veins. He was trapped. There was no way he could bypass Sykes —not now. Later, after he and his bunch had trailed and hung the Kid and Slocum. After that he'd take care of this ape who wanted to bed down his beautiful Honey.

He could see Sykes watching, trying to read his future.

Braddock smiled broadly. "Sykes, I got one thing in mind now. It's to nail those two buzzards to a high tree. After that I'll think about what you want." He grinned. "I can understand your yen for the filly. She's the kinda girl cowboys dream about. And I sure mean to give you the lead, for the reasons you said."

He turned to look at the stretch of his range. "This is a rich country. There's a big future here."

He turned and moved close to Sykes, patting his shoulder. "You go after those two dogs and stretch their necks. Then we'll talk it over. Don't mind saying I always liked the cut of you, Sykes. And I reckon the little filly does, too." His mouth twisted —trouble was that Honey seemed to like *all* men.

Sykes nodded. "She's the cutest filly I ever seen, Mr. Braddock. And I know she favors me. You won't be makin' a mistake, bringin' me in. You'll never have a rustler problem, long as I can pull a gun."

"Okay," Braddock said, looking stern, suddenly

the boss. "Now, Sykes, your job is to get those two killers. And don't stop until you do it." He stared hard into Sykes's eyes. "I'd say a lot is ridin' on you doin' this job."

Sykes frowned, then he smiled. "Mr. Braddock, the Kid and Slocum are dead men."

He walked away, and Braddock, left with the words ringing in his ears, couldn't help but smile.

Under a steamy sky, Slocum and Jane rode into rugged country, pocketed with shrubs and gnarled cedars. He tried for high ground, to give him the long view, and when they came to a rise, they dismounted. They pulled out their canteens and drank. Around them the sun hit hard on the raw cliffs.

Slocum looked up. Overhead a buzzard soared, gazing down, waiting patiently for something to die. Slocum shook his head. Hell of a way to get a dinner. A tiny lizard sprinted across a hot rock and screeched to a halt in the shade, its throat pulsing. Then it darted into a hole and disappeared.

"They're coming," Slocum said, pointing.

She could see the riders, small in the distance, riding close together.

Small Dog, probably, had picked up the trail, and they were on their way, come hell or high water.

She studied the riders. "Is Braddock with them?"

"Too far to know."

"We'll let them come and find out," she said, sipping water from her canteen. "I don't see myself running from Braddock when I should be running toward him."

Slocum nodded. "What if he's not with them?"

"Then we go for him at the ranch."

"That's what Devlin did," Slocum said. "Instead of running, he went for Braddock. He found an ace in Honey. It put him in a fine spot to bargain for his life." Slocum shook his head, remembering. "Trouble was, Devlin got bogged down by the girl, and it blunted his edge. He was looking at her when he should have been looking out for the hanging bunch. I caught him off guard."

Jane suddenly smiled. "I s'pose you're saying women are dangerous."

He looked at her face—it was so lovely, but under it she was a buzzsaw, not what you would expect. "Women are the deadlier of the species," he said. "Like you, the way you pull your gun."

There were specks of fire in her blue eyes. "I got cause. Will Braddock ride with his men?"

Slocum considered it. "He might, just to see you get a necktie party. But you're his devil. He won't want to be near the Masked Kid. You put fear in his bones."

"I hope so," she said coldly.

Braddock watched the bunch headed by Sykes ride out to track down Slocum and the Masked Kid. His misery would disappear as soon as they had the Kid hanged. He leaned against the corral fence and began to think about the Bakely ranch. He had to tie up all the loose ends.

The door of the white house opened and Honey came out in her tight pants. He stared at his daughter, a young filly with a very friendly eye for cowboys. She really needed marrying.

She waved at him and started toward her pinto. When he beckoned, she came up, looking pretty as a doe. But she had the instincts of a tigress.

"I been thinkin', Honey, it's time for you to get hitched."

She smiled. "Not a bad idea."

"No." His voice was dry. "Would you believe this? Sykes came up and said he was mighty interested."

"He did? Sykes is a nice hombre." Her eyes shone with her memories.

It made Braddock grind his teeth. "You find all men nice hombres."

She shrugged. "Maybe so. Can't help that."

He shook his head. "Daughter, you need marryin' in the worst way. What d'ya think of Curly Wilson over at the Bar-W ranch?"

She thought of his strong arms, his hard body. "I like Curly."

Braddock gritted his teeth. "Now, that cowboy is right for you. His dad's got a fine stretch of land and plenty of stock."

"Curly's a solid boy." Then, after a bit of thought she said, "Sykes might not like it. Might kick up a fuss."

Braddock nodded. "Don't worry about him." He thought of Silent Louie, who knew how to track a man, put a bullet in his back, bury him, all nice and quiet. He'd put Silent Louie on Sykes after Sykes did the hanging job on the Kid and Slocum.

"No, you just fix your mind on Curly. His dad and I been talkin' about you two."

Honey shrugged. She didn't really mind. Curly

was a rugged cowboy with broad shoulders, a big chest, and a hard body. Nights would be lots of fun with him. That was the main thing. Still, Sykes might make trouble. But her dad had a way of dealing with such things. She had confidence in him. Too bad about Sykes. He was ornery, but he sure knew how to give a girl a good time.

"Maybe I'll mosey up to the Bar-W and see what's stirring with Curly," she said.

"A fine idea," he said, thinking he had set her up with the Wilson folk, and that should take care of her future.

She turned to her pinto, then stopped. "Dad?"

The tone of her voice caught him.

"What is it about the Masked Kid that makes you foam at the mouth? He sure bothers you."

Braddock stared. She had noticed his rage and fear. Well, what was it? It was damned clear why. Because the Kid had killed Jared Cooper, Charley Amis, Luke Jones, Seth Williams—all his partners in crime. Why'd he hit just them? What did he know? How could he know? There'd been nobody there, nobody, when they did the old man in and grabbed his gold. So out of the past comes this Masked Kid, like an avenging demon, tracking just these men, not robbing, but killing them. He was a rotten mystery. And he had to be wiped out. He'd bet his ass that he himself was on the Kid's list. He was the last. The others had been gunned down. Only he was left. He felt seared by fear.

Honey was watching him, astonished at his craven look.

"The Kid is a killer," he suddenly snarled. "He's

killed my oldest sidekicks. Jared, Luke, Charley, Seth. That's why, Honey. And he's goin' to pay. Even hanging is too good for him."

He turned and looked anxiously to the slope, his last sight of his bunch.

"Get the bastard," he cursed.

As the bunch came riding toward them, Slocum and Jane, who were perched behind a clump of iron-wood on high ground, could look down on them. They could make out some of the riders.

"I don't see Braddock," Slocum said. "Reckon he's not anxious to run into you." He grinned. "Must worry the hell outa him to realize he's the last man."

"I aimed for that," she said. "I want him to feel fear." She pulled back. "Let's go to my place, then we'll try to corner Braddock."

"What about them?" he jerked his finger at the oncoming riders.

"I've no quarrel with them. Let's not get into a shoot-out with them."

"But they're out to quarrel with us." He pulled his rifle from his saddle holster. "Maybe I can discourage them a little." He fired, and the dust spurted in front of the first horse, which reared up, almost dislodging its rider.

The bunch, aware of a bushwhacker with a fine eye, raced their horses for cover. Slocum fired a few more shots to speed them on.

He watched, then said, "Let's ride."

"They may keep coming."

"We'll know they're serious then," he said.

She glanced at him. "They're fond of hanging. That's serious."

He nodded. "If they're thinking that, then it's either them or us." Stroking his chin thoughtfully, he said, "Sykes is going to be serious. Because he's got ambitions."

She turned to him. "Like what?"

"Sykes wants Braddock as his father-in-law."

She looked grim. "He wants Honey? They almost deserve each other. But I've got Braddock in mind. Once we take care of him, the bunch will melt away. Let's try not to tangle with them."

He stared down. "Only way I know is to disable Small Dog. Or put Sykes out of business. The others couldn't track their way out of a sack of potatoes."

"Let's do it, then." She took the rifle out of its saddle holster. "You take Sykes, I'll take Small Dog."

They waited behind the clumped ironwood, and before long the bunch regrouped and again started up the hill. They had hanging in mind, all right, Slocum thought grimly.

Small Dog took the lead, with Sykes following. When Slocum felt the shooting could be accurate, he signaled Jane, and they both raised their rifles. The sound of their shots echoed against the cliffs as two men fell from their horses. Not hit fatally, they crawled for cover. The other riders again scattered, fearful of such deadly shooting.

"That stopped them," Slocum said.

Mounting up, they rode southwest, working a big

circle toward the Bakely ranch. Once they stopped at a stream to water the horses.

"When we reach our ranch, I'll pick up some clothes," Jane said, "then we'll start for Braddock's."

"Might be the end of the trail," said Slocum.

Sure in his mind that Sykes and his boys would take care of the Kid and Slocum, Braddock could now put his mind to the Bakelys. It was time to clinch the deal on that ranch. He wanted it to spread his ranch west, and because he needed more water for his cattle.

For a long time he'd craved Bakely's ranch and had almost buffaloed Martha into selling until her niece, Jane, came there to live. That damned filly had spoiled it all.

When Slats came to him about scaring the hell outa the filly, he'd almost bought the idea. But if it got out, it'd be bad. He'd decided to ride over now and give them the final warning: buy or else.

Yes, it was showdown time for the Bakelys. If they turned him down he'd bring in Silent Louie, a slimy, skinny gunslinger on his payroll who knew how to quietly make his enemies disappear.

His face was grim as he rode toward the Bakelys. Yes, it was time to tie up all the loose knots—the Kid, Slocum, and the Bakelys, too.

They reached the Bakely ranch near sunset. The sky was streaked with crimson and orange. The ranch looked serene, a fine stretch of smooth, richly green grass.

They went into the house, where Jane poured them both cold cider.

"Aunt Martha is on a visit to Mrs. Malcom, one of her dear friends, in the west valley," Jane said. "We're alone."

It was then that she looked through the window and, to her astonishment, saw Braddock riding toward the ranch. Her eyes widened almost with shock. Again she thought of how the hand of God moved in mysterious ways. But why was Braddock coming? Why shouldn't he? He wanted the land, didn't he? He'd come to talk, even make a final offer. She looked at her vest and pants. "I'll change and see him as Jane Bakely."

"What's he come for?"

"To make an offer, probably, before he tells his gunslingers to clear away the women."

"That's nice. And what will you do?" Slocum asked.

"What do you think?" Her smile was deadly. Her enemy had stumbled in her lair. But he was dangerous, too.

Braddock swung off his horse and stood bulky, arrogant, looking around the land. As if he already owned it, she thought.

When she came out, he said, "Hello, Miss Bakely. I've come to talk to your Aunt Martha."

"Visiting a neighbor?" She stared at him, the man who had murdered her father. Her rage was deep, but she concealed it. "What do you want?"

He turned and waved his arm at the broad, smooth land. "Want? I want this. I want to expand my spread. I need your stream. And I'm here to

make you Bakelys a fine offer. Eight hundred dollars. You can't get better than that." His eyes glinted like steel. "I think it'd be smart of you Bakelys to take it."

"No," she said. "I don't think we'll take it."

He stared rudely at her. "Stubborn little critter. You're the reason your aunt is crossing me. She was willin' enough before you barged in and spoiled everything. An outsider. You're an outsider. A spoiler."

Her eyes gleamed, and she smiled.

It startled him, infuriated him. He thought of Slats, who'd come to him with an idea about the Bakely filly. He was sorry he hadn't given Slats the go-ahead to scare them off the land.

"Look, lady, I've run out of patience. The time for talk is over. I'll send someone. They won't be polite." Glaring at her, he turned toward his horse.

"Just a minute, Braddock," her voice was cool. "I might reconsider. Give me a moment. I'll be right back."

He kicked at the earth, furious with the insolent hussy. A pretty filly, but headed for a dead end. He knew how to handle his enemies. He thought again of Silent Louie, who did his dirty jobs.

He turned to look at the land, so rich, and already he felt he owned it.

"Braddock."

He was startled by the voice behind him. It was low but somehow familiar, and it had a cutting edge.

He whirled around. His brown eyes shocked open.

It was the Masked Kid.

The Kid wore his black mask, dark pants, and yellow vest. His gun was in its holster. And behind him stood Slocum.

Braddock felt ice in his veins. His worst fears had materialized—The Masked Kid facing him. How in hell did the bunch let them get through?

Braddock's nerve failed him. But the Kid was doing nothing, just staring at him with glowing blue eyes through the holes in the mask.

He sweated, and tried to nerve himself up. "Who the hell are you? Why do you wear that mask? Why don't you show yourself?"

"Oh, I'll do that. Soon enough."

They stared at each other.

Then Braddock, who had to know, said. "Why'd you kill Jared, Luke, and the others? What had they done to you?"

"The same thing you did to me."

Braddock took a deep breath. Could this sonofabitch know something? No, it was impossible. "What the hell do you mean? What did we do?"

"You killed my father."

Braddock stared in disbelief. "You must be loco. Don't know you or your father." He paused. "So all this time you've been on a crazy run for revenge."

The Kid said nothing for a moment, then: "How'd you get the money for your ranch, Braddock?"

Braddock paled. Somehow this kid knew something, but it didn't make sense. How could he know. "What do you mean?" he blustered. "How the hell do you s'pose I got it?"

"Well, since you won't tell me, I'll tell you. You bought it with gold that you stole from an old miner."

Braddock just stared. This was impossible, he was dreaming. Nobody had been there.

"Yes," the Masked Kid went on. "You and your rotten sidekicks came one day to an old cabin and surrounded an old miner who had sweated and suffered for years to dig gold. And when he finally got it, you stole it. Even after he offered it, you killed him."

Braddock went limp inside. "You're plumb loco."

"I was there."

"That's a lie," Braddock hissed, then he flushed. The wrong thing to say. How could he say it was a lie unless he'd been there.

The blue eyes burned behind the mask. "I was in the cellar. I saw it all."

Braddock's flesh crawled. So that was it. The Kid had seen it happen. From the cellar. Now he remembered: someone had said, "There's supposed to be a kid." But who could have dreamed that the kid had been hiding in the cellar, had seen his father killed in cold blood. So that he'd been on a track of revenge for a killing that happened years ago. And now the Kid was here for the showdown. Braddock felt the chill in his blood: he was last on the list. He had to use his wits, there must be a way, he had always prepared for a moment like this. Suddenly his spirits lifted. He still had a card to play.

"It was my father you killed, you greedy bas-

tard," the Kid said. "And this is your day of reckoning."

"What do you mean?"

The Kid then said, "Slocum, if I don't kill him, you do it."

Slocum smiled.

Braddock suddenly threw his gun on the floor. Then he straightened up with a yellow smile. "I'm not goin' to shoot. And you won't either. You always made the others draw. Well, I won't."

There was a long silence.

"Pick up your gun or I'll shoot you down like a dog," the Kid said.

Braddock studied the Kid. "No, I don't believe you. You're not that kind."

Slocum's jaw tightened. Braddock was a sly dog. What did he have in mind?

"Who the hell are you?" Braddock suddenly demanded. "Why do you hide behind that mask? Let's see what you look like."

There was a long moment of silence. Then the Kid's hand went slowly up to the mask and lifted it.

Braddock stared in disbelief. Jane Bakely! What the hell did it mean? So all this time it had been Bakely. As a young girl, she had seen her father killed. And she had trained for years for revenge. Now she finally had him on target.

The sweat broke out on his face. If only he'd looked in that cellar. Too late. Somehow he felt less threatened because it was Jane, a girl, facing him. Not the terrible, mysterious Masked Kid, who seemed invincible.

It was a young girl. Why was he in a sweat? He just had to be smart.

"I'm not goin' to shoot a girl," he said.

Her jaw tightened. "Pick up that gun or I'll shoot you like the rattler you are."

Braddock shook his head. "Not goin' to shoot a girl, not goin' to pick up my gun. You'll have to kill me in cold blood."

When Jane, perplexed, turned to Slocum, wondering what to do, Braddock made his move with the back-up derringer always carried in his sleeve. It was suddenly in his hand, and he brought it up quick to shoot first her, then Slocum.

Slocum's hand moved in a blur so fast Braddock never saw it, just felt the bullet and the sudden pain in his gut. Braddock jumped, wilted, and fell on his back to the floor.

His eyes were on Jane Bakely. She looked anguished, because she'd been robbed of her revenge. But he was still alive. She shook her auburn hair, so that it flowed around her head. This young woman, whose father he had killed. She stared down, aware that he was still conscious, and brought her gun up slowly. In his mind's eye, with terrible vividness, Braddock saw the old miner on the floor, even as the gun in the Kid's hand barked and spouted fire. The bullet struck his heart.

Braddock's body jumped. His eyes stayed on Jane until finally they went empty.

For a few moments, Jane stared at his body. Then all the rage that for years had burned like a live coal in her heart seemed suddenly to go out. A look of peace came over her lovely face. Her eyes

misted, and she turned to Slocum. She came close, leaned on his chest, put her arms around him, and reached up to kiss his mouth.

Slocum smiled. He'd give her what she needed, then move on.

His job here was finished.

JAKE LOGAN

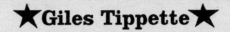

OTHER BOOKS BY JAKE LOGAN

SHOOTOUT!

There was no way Slocum could pull his gun and have time to turn and shoot. Moose went for his gun. But Slocum had kept one eye in the mirror. His move was pure speed; his left hand pulled his gun, and, without turning, he twisted to shoot under his armpit, firing twice, his bullets crashing into Moose, tearing open his chest.

Moose's eyes were wide with shock at what had happened. He kept staring, then, aware that Slocum had outguessed and outgunned him, fell with a curse. He lay on the floor, twisting in agony as his heart's blood poured out. He kept staring up at Slocum.

"May you rot in hell," he whispered.

Then he died.